G R JORDAN

The Blasphemous Welcome

Dark Wen Book 1

*To the writers on the island, especially Chris, Hereward, Dave and
never forgotten Chrisella,*

*For the joy that only comes from sharing our wonder of the art and
the tales of the wayward pen!*

Contents

Acknowledgement

To my wife and our kids for letting me explore these bizarre worlds that occupy my mind. Life sure is busy with you all but would be so much less without you.

To Carl at Extended Imagery for keeping at the cover until we got just what we wanted.

To Roma, for her honesty, insight and editing skills, it's been a great partnership.

To all the writers out there in online land who give of their advice, time and energy in commenting on my covers and books. There really are some truly giving people out there.

To the coffee shops of the Isle of Lewis, well, what would life be without them!

To God for the everful watchful eye and guiding hand.

1

Chapter 1

This is good coffee. I mean that quite seriously, this is good coffee. It's not that Java muck that's brutal on your tongue, over brewed and an assault of flavour, so strong you can't even taste it. No, this is smooth and has just a hint of a chocolate undertone. Maybe Kenya or Costa Rica. Like I would know. But it is good coffee.

You might be wondering why this means so much to me. Here I am, sitting at a metal table, a bloody grimy one at that, and staring out at all the people running here there and everywhere. Every single one of them in a damn rush. I should be in a rush too, but hey, I can't think about that just now. You see, she said I had to take my moments of peace and serenity. The little ponds of calm. Who said it? Why, Jessica, my little island of sanity in this daft world.

I started seeing her—no can't say that, can I?—or you might get the wrong idea. No, I started going to her about six months ago. She's a counsellor, a shrink you might say, but she would give me a right dirty look if I said that in front of her. She's like a sounding board, an outlet for my bitterness, turning it into positivity. Ah bollocks, that's a bit overboard. Well, she helps me tune out the crap and hold on to the real scoop out there. Tidy figure too for her age. Lucky guy at home. Although you never can tell, she's paid to be nice to me.

Who's me? Me is Detective Kyle Mulgrew Trimble, once of homicide, twice of narcotics and now of special detachment after the incident. A long time bringer of good and hope to this crappy city. You can hear the sarcasm, right? Sometimes you Yanks don't get sarcasm. And I lay it on pretty thick. It's my upbringing, how I was reared. A right wee hellion. God rest her soul, she hauled me up knowing right from wrong and how to avoid the fall if I got it wrong. Ten years, Mum, ten long years.

I was saying this coffee is damn good and it's served by Karen, the stick insect. At least that's what a lot of the regulars call her, and it's dammed unfair in my opinion. What do I know? Well, I'm a man so I come with the tools to assess women and like the rest of my kind, I find myself volunteering in this aspect. Sorry girls, you got the looks, we got the binos. Hell, that sounds creepy. Scratch that.

Karen's actually really nice. Yes, she's thin and not exactly voluptuous, one of those girls not blessed with womanly curves. But, hey, she suits her figure, and she's a sweet girl too. Very pleasant face. Got a brain too and knows how to use it. So why's she serving coffee, you ask? Student, earning her keep. And keeping her nose clean, which in a city like this is a major effort. The number of her kind I see parading on stage and shooting up. In my professional capacity, of course.

She's just lifted my mug which is probably my cue for getting this day underway. My boss has already tried to ring my mobile five times, and frankly, he can shove it up his ass. He's getting his knickers in a twist as there's been a major homicide downtown and the press dogs are all over it. I called Lewanski on the desk after the first three calls and it's a biggie alright. Someone broke into the Giardelli's mansion and blew the three brothers away. Nasty pieces of work shafted by an even nastier piece of work. Bodies and blood everywhere. And the boss with his knickers in a twist. Well, I couldn't give a damn as I have a woman to meet.

Ah, now you're interested. What's she like? Well, I don't know yet as she's only getting in today. All I know is she's called Kyla Corstain, she's a relatively new detective at twenty-five, and she's just been through a pretty shitty time. That's why she's transferring from down south. And as she's broken, no one wants her. So she's with me on the specials, 'cause I'm broke too. Anyway, I'm going to be late if I don't get my ass in gear.

I take the subway across town to the Grand station, where she's arriving on the night train at 08:05. Part of me would rather drive as at least it's air conditioned, but the roads are hell at this time. So, instead, I make a vague run towards and catch the underground sweat box with the silent people and their papers. Like the rest, I'm wearing a rather dapper hat and a long trench coat as upstairs it's positively Baltic. Yes, I do like my coffee in the cool air, thanks for asking. I hate the subway, standing inches from these soulless morons with their briefcases and smart ties. I'm forty now, and I don't want a damn tie.

The Grand station is absolutely heaving as I clamber up the stairs from the subway, scanning to see a platform for her train. Electronic screens change so quickly, and I almost lose sight of the update of her train as it flashes from one screen to another.

Platform eleven. I take just a brief moment to admire the world's largest chandelier, hanging above me on an impossibly strong cable. Thousands of little pieces of crystal reflecting the bright light around the magnificent hall. Stunningly beautiful and strangely beyond these cretans view. If you want to show beauty in this town, you need to slam it in someone's face.

Ducking down a narrow stairwell, I stand at the end of platform eleven as a long rumbling train grinds to a halt. Gradually doors open and weary looking punters emerge, most with a ridiculous number of bags and cases. Porters run to assist, and I look along the train for a twenty-five-year-old refugee. There's a woman standing in a smart skirt and blouse, trim and neat, and getting some serious attention. But that's not her, Kyla is dark on top with a bit of a tan. Still, I had to check.

"Detective Trimble?"

The voice comes from behind, and it's a little unsure, not altogether confident. I turn around and look straight into two very dark eyes framed by long black hair. There's a hand extended, and I take it firmly, shaking it. Her skin is certainly tanned, almost heading towards dark brown, and she seems to be struggling to hold my gaze. She dressed in trainers, jeans, green t-shirt and a denim jacket. Unlike Karen, she fills them without looking like she's forced herself into them.

"Hi. Yes, I'm Detective Kyle Mulgrew Trimble. But as we're working together, you can call me Mulgrew. Only my partner gets to call me that."

"Okay, thanks." She's still shaking my hand. Poor kid, she's nervous, and no wonder, looking at this mess of an overworked, overtired curmudgeon in front of her.

"And I call you what?"

"Detective Kyla Corstain."

"Little formal, don't you think?"

"Sorry didn't sleep much."

"That's alright. But what do I call you?"

"At the last place it was Corstain."

"Well to hell with those memories, nice to meet you Kyla. You got a bag or anything?"

She shook her head, and I couldn't help notice her hair flounce briefly, exposing her neck. This was my partner, and I was trying to be professional and detached yet warm and friendly, however that works. But I'm a man and she was in the binos sights. Yeah, it's still creepy.

"Got stolen through the night. 'Fraid this is it."

"Well, here," I said, passing her a badge with the precinct on it, "time to make a fresh start. The biggest crime family in town just got blown away, so I'm afraid it's going to be straight in at the deep end. We'll get round to sorting out the baggage later. You carrying?"

She shook her head again and damn did I try and not look at her neck.

"Okay Kyla, we'll drop by the station and get you a firearm. You don't take chances in this city."

"And I need a hotel."

"Later. Time to work."

2

Chapter 2

"Who's the broad, Trimble?"

Broad? Obviously the diversity training taken on by the force isn't working with the Chief. He's a bit of an old relic, a couple of months from retirement, and yes, a living cliché that the commissioner wants rid of. Modern policing and the Chief don't sit side by side. He missed the whole woman's lib movement. But hey, he's actually a good guy and a pretty decent policeman. That's high praise from me, by the way. I don't do praise that often.

"This lady is my new partner, Chief. Let me introduce Detective Corstain, newly arrived on this morning's sleeper."

"So you ditched my calls for a pick-up run? Shit, Trimble, this is a big deal we're looking at here. There's going to be a mob war if we're not careful."

Mob war? The man is a relic. There aren't any mobs in the city, just ruthless families and businessmen operating with sod all loyalty. Not that I think the mobs had any class. A killer is a killer in my book. And a rip off merchant is a scamster. I don't care how they dress or whose ass they are up.

"Sorry to be a bother," says Kyla, and she is suddenly not the nervous, unconfident young woman I collected from the station. She displays her piece on her hip, I guess purely for the Chief's benefit. I can see him eyeing her up and down, but she keeps a calm face that says "In your dreams!" But there's a uniform interrupting with some paperwork, and I take the chance to step aside with Kyla.

"Look, I'm sure you know your way about, but this place we are standing in is kinda important. The bodies in the next room, well, three of them anyway, had fingers in every cream pie going in this town, and that means there will be plenty of interested parties. Not a place to make a foul-up just because you're new in town. So just follow my lead, okay?" She nods, and I'm hoping I didn't seem like a patronising parent. She reaches behind her head, gathering up her thick hair and ties it in a pony tail. Yes, that neck is something.

"Smart and professional Mulgrew. Is this okay?"

"Come on. You'll do."

We had come up to the north side of town to an area I can't afford a bus in, never mind a house. We picked up the department's wheels, and I let Kyla drive, supposedly to let her settle in, but in reality I wanted to see if she could drive. I've been a city guy for the last thirty years, and I drive like Miss Daisy. But she seemed confident.

The Marconi district has residents who never use a bus or even drive their own cars. There aren't houses here but palaces and security the US government can't afford. Normally the police don't make calls here unless invited, but a certain uninvited guest had made our presence tolerable, if not welcome. I recognise some figures from the Giradellis' outfit, all here no doubt to stake a claim for leadership now that the snake's head had been removed.

I take Kyla aside and give her a brief rundown of the Giradelli family history. Their father had been a small time crook but had swam with the big fishes until he had learnt his trade well enough to one day flush them down the toilet. For twenty years he had maintained a front with the political elite whilst running major rackets in extortation, money laundering and general death. Then, one day, his sons had taken him out to the gorge and executed him. I'm sure he was proud that his sons had learnt the family way so well.

Of all the players in the city, the Giradellis were the biggest and most potent. And someone had simply waltzed into their fortress and taken them out. There's bound to be a lot of nervous criminals in town at the moment.

"Shall we look at the damage, boss?"

Boss! No-one calls me Boss, least of all my partner.

"Told you, it's Mulgrew. I ain't your boss. Just your partner."

"But you are the senior detective?"

"Listen Kyla, out there all we got is thee and me. So we are partners, okay? Always partners."

"Okay. So who's the man we need to talk to, partner?"

I gave a slight wave to indicate to her to follow me and walked into a room of busy activity. There's always something surreal about a murder scene, and this was no different. Men and women in white plastic throw-away suits worked painstakingly at various minutiae around the room. There were little yellow markers with numbers on them. Plastic bags were at a premium and being sealed like they would soon be out of fashion. And then I see her. Jenny Tatler, one of the best forensic technicians I had ever worked with and also one of the most tragic.

"Jen, how are things?"

"Mulgrew, you dipstick. I'm up to my eyes or can't you tell? You always were a crap detective."

The white plastic hood is removed once she has stepped away from her work and reveals a sharp face with barely a blemish. Forty-something and wearing so much better than me. Even her blonde hair is still immaculate.

"Let me introduce Detective Kyla Corstain. Kyla, this is Jenny Tatler. The, and I mean *the*, best forensic investigator I have ever worked with."

"You big smuck. I hope he didn't hit on you, Kyla."

Kyla steps out from behind me and reaches out with her right hand to shake, but Jen doesn't oblige. It takes a moment before Kyla notices Jen's missing arm. I did say tragic.

"Sorry," says Kyla, issuing her left hand forth now and engaging in rather a limp shake.

"It's okay. Long time ago, and a story for another day. Now I guess you'll want a run down."

"You know me," I say, "the basics and none of the irrelevance you give the Chief."

"Hey, I get paid for my irrelevance!" Jen smiles, and I see the rosy lips that I once tasted so many years ago. They say some people never leave you, and Jen's mark is still carried on my breast. If it hadn't have been for Hope…well, another long story.

"As you can see," begins Jen, "our perpetrator wasn't too subtle. And you are looking at the sanitised version. We already pieced the brothers together from different corners of the room. In total, there's nine dead, the three brothers and six so-called protectors. Now as you can see, there's plenty of bullet holes in the walls but none in the victims. I'm betting that ballistics is going to trace every bullet to a gun in here. All the victims were slashed in some form, with a weapon unknown."

"A blade, a sword?" I venture.

"Unknown, but certainly a clean edge. But that's not all. Look at Thomas Giradelli. That's the one pinned to the wall, Kyla. As far as I can tell, and this is provisional, but he was dead before he was ripped apart."

"From what," asks Kyla, "drugged?"

"No. Fright."

"Fright? That brutal bastard?" I ask.

"Yes, fright. Terror. I'm betting he wasn't touched until he was dead."

"Who could scare him to death?" I ask, shaking my head. "He was the animal of the group, the terroriser. As far as I knew, he was nails."

"Hey, I only tell you what happened. That's why the Chief was dancing around when you wouldn't answer. There's something funny going on here."

"Jen, may I?" Kyla's kneeling down now at a bag on the floor, the contents of which are a head. Well, she's not squeamish. "Who's this?"

"One of the bodyguards, Mexican by birth, I believe."

"But he's white, sheer white."

"Yes, I know."

"Keep this under wraps, Jen. Until we can attribute this to something." I say. I don't really like bodies, especially ones which have been so massively dis-assembled. Time for another coffee.

"Time to go, Kyla. I need some lunch. Keep us posted, Jen."

"Will do."

"But Mulgrew…" says Kyla.

"What?"

"This face. Not the actual face…but this terror…this whitening of the face. I've seen it before."

3

Chapter 3

I haul Kyla to one side and ask her, "What do you mean you've seen this before?"

"Well, I have. Back up country where I used to work. There was a case regarding a pretty nasty murder. And the face of the deceased looked liked that. White as a sheet, eyes wide in terror."

I gaze at her face, looking to see if she's trying to take centre stage here. Maybe as she's just blown in she wants to make a mark for herself. This is not the time to do it. Personally, I really don't want to be in the middle of this one as there's going to be repercussions all over the city. And I'd rather not be caught up in it.

"Any other similarities, Kyla?"

"No. It was perpetrated by a group of teenagers into all that witchcraft and the like. Whatever prank they played on the poor guy had him scared out of his wits before they murdered him. They tried to say it wasn't them and gave some cock and bull story about incantations and all that, but their prints were everywhere." She smiles being the dutiful partner passing on something they know. I'll give her the benefit of the doubt.

"And could these teenagers be involved here, do you think?"

"No," she says, very definitively, "I doubt they would even have been set free yet. It was only five years ago. I was just starting out on the job, wasn't really my case, just a helpful uniform that day."

I give it a moment's thought and then head back to the Chief. He's surrounded by some of the homicide guys, all looking a little perplexed and a lot worried. In the background, I can see some of the Giradelli family. Their faces look like they need someone to blame and fast.

"Chief, there's not much else I can do here except let the forensics go through it. Seems like there's little here. Did they have any footage of the incident?"

The Chief barely acknowledges me and taps a beefy looking detective on the shoulder and points at me. The dark-haired muscleman takes me to one side.

"What do you need, Detective?"

Good, he's one of the clever ones. The Chief doesn't let information flow out here and there easily. This guy's recognised I'm in the inner circle. Must keep an eye on him.

"What's your name, son?"

"Haskins, sir. How can I help?"

"Did they have any video footage? I mean, of all the houses, this one has to have security."

He nods. "There's footage alright. Got tapes and tapes of the last twenty-four hours. They cover every single room or piece of ground except that room."

"The killing room then. Taken out in their own killing room."

"About time those bastards took a hit, sir."

"Keep that to yourself, Detective. Pretty soon this city's going to light up if we don't get on top of this one. But you're right, I won't miss them."

He gives a grunt and then tells me the name of the officer working through the tapes back at the station. After a nod for his efforts, I call Kyla over. She's been pottering around, hopefully not pissing off forensics.

"Well, find anything?"

She grins and then turns to scan the room. I catch the side of her neck and face. Very passable. Not the most generous comment, but she's my partner and I can't afford to be generous.

"I've never seen anything like this. Look at the mayhem around here. You have nine guys with serious weaponry, obviously attacked, and then giving a defence our military would be proud of, and yet every single one of them is dead. But as for the killer, nothing. No marks, hair, pieces of clothing. In a scrap like this, you'd expect something. Anything?"

She's right. There should be something. And she's right, one killer. All the wounds seem to be made with the same weapon. A blade of some kind.

"How did he dodge the bullets? Nine guys, plenty of bullets in the walls. How?"

"You got me, Mulgrew. It'd be like something from a cartoon."

I tell Kyla about the video and suggest we head back to the station. I insist she drives again and get her to drive past Jimmy's coffee house on 17th. She chooses an espresso, and I watch her throw it down quickly. My latte is going to be a while longer, but I encourage her to drive on. As we pull into the station, there's a horde of media.

We step out of the car, and I have a microphone thrust in my face.

"Detective, can you inform us…"

"No comment."

"But surely you must have something?"

"Yeah, they faked the moon landing but that's gotta wait. Think there's something bigger happening."

I can hear Kyla giggle as I say this. and for some reason I feel glad that she's impressed. That's how it started before. And look how that finished. But she looks pretty when she smiles.

The whole precinct is in overdrive. Various department heads can be heard shouting at junior officers, and it seems every Tom, Dick and Harry is into this murder. I show Kyla the way down to the techies on the base level and then over to Kurt, or Officer Sulliven as he's meant to be known. At only thirty years of age, Kurt still has his looks, blonde locks and a body that's honed tight—or so the girls in the precinct say. The poor guy kinda thinks he owes me one after a prank some of the guys played on him. You see, Kurt prefers men, and well if you haven't guessed yet, I like women. But they told him different, and he went for it hook, line and sinker. There were gifts and looks and then an abrupt conversation. I didn't blame him, and he's a good guy to know. To this day, I don't know how I feel about his affections for me. Apart from being disinterested, that is.

"How's the best looking officer in the Division?"

Kurt looks up and smiles. I always hit him with that one, seems to make him less embarrassed about before. He glances behind me, and then gives me a flash of his eyes to say, "I see you hooked a right one". I give a little shake of the head.

"This is my new partner, Kurt. Meet detective Kyla Corstain."

"Oh, yes, pleased Ma'am." They shake hands, and Kurt begins to inform us of how the precinct has gone silly over the recent developments. The man speaks like a juggernaut being pursued, and it takes a concerted period of hand waving to silence him.

"I need Rathman. They said I need Rathman."

Kurt smiles and then turns and points to a desk in the far corner which has a multitude of screens surrounding it. I let Kyla walk ahead of me, and I can see glances in her direction from all around the room. Now, that's not saying a lot in our precinct. I mean, she's female. That's all it takes. Well, except for Kurt, of course.

Rathman turns out to be a dumpy Mexican woman of maybe fifty years of age. She has thick black hair and is tightly contained by her uniform. She's also a hired specialist and not an officer and looks at us accusingly from behind a pair of thick glasses.

"Yes?"

"Sorry to trouble you, Ma'am, but we were directed to you regarding the Giradelli incident. They said you were checking the footage from the house." Kyla has quite an engaging tone, unlike me, and I can see Rathman's frostiness melt in the warmth of Kyla's parlance. I'll sit this one out.

"Why, my dear? Anything in particular?"

"We were wondering have you seen anything unusual. Anything untoward? Any perpetrator entering?"

Rathman shakes her head. "I've been scanning this footage since I came in. They have heat as well as the ordinary alarm trips too. There's been no one entering that room. There was no one else in that room from the video. All day, only the bodyguards and the Giradelli brothers, and none of them eventually left. But I'll tell you this, they don't use that room much."

"What makes you say that?" asks Kyla.

"Well, no one was in it for most of the day, and then they all assemble there."

"So, they seemed purposeful when entering?"

"I believe so," says Rathman.

"How sure are you that these pictures are genuine?" I interrupt.

"Are you questioning my competence?" Rathman has now raised her shoulders and looks like a mini rhino.

"No. On the contrary," I say, "I was merely asking if there could have been any tampering of the footage or of the camera taking the footage."

"I don't see anything untoward. Do you need me to clarify that?"

"Yes, I do. Here's my number."

I hand over my card and give a brief thank you before exiting. Kyla follows me, and I take the elevator to the roof. She doesn't make a sound in the lift and then stands with me on the edge of the roof looking out over the city.

"Okay, Kyla, impress me. The Giradellis are in there for a meeting, but no one comes in or out. There's a killfest without a perpetrator, and no one walks away. Cameras cover the exits. Where's our killer?"

Kyla stands, hand now on her chin like she learnt how to think from an acting class. She knows I'm watching her, but she's giving out no sign. Now there's a slight lifting of her right eyebrow, faint, but it's there. There's a grin. She turns to me now beaming with her success.

"Mulgrew, if you had a kill room and lots of cameras, the cameras would be there to show nothing had happened. Nothing had entered. But if you did take someone in then you would have another entrance."

"Exactly! Wanna bet there's no house schematics."

4

Chapter 4

We're back at the Giradelli mansion where forensics have finished to a significant degree. The place has been showered in photographs all winging their way downtown, and the significant quantities of blood have been removed. Despite this, Kyla and I are wearing contamination suits provided by the lovely Jenny Tatler.

Jen isn't too impressed by our theory as she's just gone over the entire room with a fine tooth comb. She's giving me one of her questioning looks as if I am up to something else. Given our history, that's entirely understandable. Kyla ignores any looks we are getting and proceeds to start tapping the walls.

"It's logical that there's a false door in one of these walls," says Kyla, hands frisking the nearest wall.

"Hardly dear," rebuffs Jenny, we have been all round these walls getting bullets out of them. We'd have found any false partitions. And besides, the walls look a good fit to their projected dimensions."

I have no idea what she is on about, but keep my head down regardless. So it's not the walls.

"What about the floor, Jenny? Could there be a hole in the floor?"

Jenny looks at me and gives me a sigh.

"Basically, you want the carpet up, don't you? Is there ever a crime scene you don't want ripped to shreds? I mean, just say when."

Jenny stomps off to a colleague, and I can tell she's pretty pissed at me. They will have to remove the furniture and then get the carpet up. And all this on a hunch. My hunch. But then that's what it's all about sometimes. When you got nowhere to go in this job then you take a hunch and run with it. If it works then soak it up, if not, put it down to just a stab in the dark.

Kyla has stepped clear as Jen's team get to work. They take out a stately bureau, hat stand, a ridiculously large sofa, a drinks cabinet and a desk. With all the furniture gone they roll up the carpet from one side to the other. Jen begins to walk around the floor boards sounding them out followed by Kyla.

I'm left just admiring the rather fetching light in the centre of the room. It has several lights coming off it and is hanging down by a wire from the ceiling. It must only clear a reasonable sized man by a foot or two. Still, the artwork on each of the lights is exquisite, gorgeous running lines from the brush. Well, that's the sort of thing an art buff would say about it, so why not me?

"Well that's your floorboards checked, Detective. Nothing. I guess you owe me and the boys a round after all that effort."

Jen's standing with her one hand on her hip, giving me a cheeky grin. She's thrown her head back, and I can see she's up for a bit of messing with each other.

"What do you want now, Mulgrew?" Kyla's also has her hands on her hips. I am looking away concentrating on the light as it's the only thing in the room that's not about to hit me with some sarcastic remark. It still looks rather low, certainly not where I would have put it…"

"I want you to get clear," I say, but I don't wait for them to get clear. It's a little more than a running jump, but I have a grip like a condemned man before the chair. Leaping up, I grab the light in both hands and suddenly feel myself dropping, but the light is still in my hands. Instead, the ceiling slips down until it forms a ladder up into the roof.

"Well, I'll be damned, "says Jenny, hands still on hips.

I try to step onto the ladder into the roof, but I get cuffed by Jenny, and this time it's not a playful tap.

"Where do you think you're going?"

"Up there to find out where it goes to." I give Jenny one of my determined looks, but she knows I'm in the wrong.

"Get right out of it. You're going nowhere near it until my boys have had a good run at it."

"And how long is that going to be?"

"Well," she says, "I think the day shift is going to be a night shift. Wanna stick around for a little night time action?"

Kyla raises here eyebrows at this, but then she doesn't know our past. Jenny was quite a girl back then but then I was quite a guy. Well, reasonable anyway.

"You couldn't handle a night shift with me," I tease back.

"Well, you always snored," Jenny laughs, "so it must be the midnight wanderings that make you difficult now."

I give her a look which I hope says you couldn't handle me but which probably just looks a bit dumb. She would always win our banter back then. Guess nothing much changes.

"Got things to do but I am going to stick my head up and make sure no one's up there." After a quick scout I realise there's nothing, just a way out.

"Come on Kyla," I say, "we'd better let these experts do their tidying up. Let's go see what the street says."

As we walk outside to the car, Kyla asks me what the deal is with Jenny and me.

"Just an old flame that still burns. She's a good friend after all these years, Kyla. Good friends can be difficult to find in this city, everyone looking out for themselves. But Jenny's one of the good ones. When you can't make your partner breathless anymore you start to just care. I guess me and Jenny started that a bit early."

I motion Kyla to drive again, but she isn't looking, instead taking it for granted that she is the driver. As I sit down in the passenger seat, I see she hasn't put the keys in the ignition. Instead, she's just staring out of the windscreen. In fairness, now that the night has fallen, the view out from the mansion's high position is pretty stunning, but I doubt Kyla's seeing it.

"You okay?" I ask.

"Yeah, just a bit of a whirlwind day to start. You know, Mulgrew."

"I know. But you don't have to pretend. Just say no. I'll leave it when you don't wanna talk but just call it."

She nods and gives a brief smile. "Sure. Will do. And no, I'm not and I don't want to talk about it."

"Cool. Then let's roll before they shut the bars."

"I thought we were going to the street?"

"We are. After a house call first. Edelweiss district. I'll guide you!"

5

Chapter 5

Edelweiss, such a lovely name for the city's crappiest district. It was here that I walked my first beat. Here that I grew my distrust for the human condition. And here that my view of humanity was also saved. The devils and the angels live side by side in Edelweiss.

There's a man in Edelweiss that I used to have a lot of dealings with. It's been a number of years since I last spoke to him, and in truth, there weren't a lot of words. He reacted badly to some advice I gave him and then he ran into my fist and lost a few teeth. But my advice was good, and I'm sure he'll have forgiven me. I wouldn't go to him normally as he was once my grass, and no snitch likes to see their handler unannounced.

At my instruction, Kyla pulls up in front of a semi-ruined building and steps out onto the street scanning. It's a back street, and the building has a damp smell coming from it, but then looks can be deceiving. The key thing here is to look down, not up. There's a battered door hanging off some supposedly loose catches, but I surprise Kyla by kicking the door several times.

Given the apparent state of the door, it should have collapsed in a moment, but it remains resolute. There is a small sliding hatch, maybe large enough for a pair of eyes to see out. Kyla is looking at me with raised eyebrows again. I'm beginning to think she may not trust me.

The hatch opens, and small beady eyes look out.

"Yeah?" says a voice. It's quite high pitched.

"Tell Salco his goods are here and to get his butt up here now or I'll sell to the Japanese instead."

"And just who the frig are you?"

"Just tell him the trees are a shaking. He'll know."

The little hatch slams shut, and I can hear the owner of the eyes hurry away. Kyla's looking at me, questioning if I think the chat was successful. I raise my shoulders slightly but I know he'll come.

The door bursts open, and a small man with balding black hair shuffles out followed by a number of goons. They are all holding automatic weapons, the smaller hand held variety, vainly disguised by their long jackets.

I go to speak, but the small man motions me through the ruins at the side of the house. Nodding my approval, I walk first, followed by Kyla and then the rest of our current company. It's only when I get to the passage that links the back yards of the buildings does the small man speak.

"Clifton, I didn't expect to see you."

Clifton was my contact name for the small man. His name was Salazar Coatbridges. I think his parents had gotten really excited at the birth of their one and only. Everyone shortened it to Salco. Salco was a man that moved things about for people who wanted things moved quietly. To do this, you need to know everything, lest you step on toes that bite. Hence, when we had him on laundering charges, he turned grass. But he had kept it quiet.

"What's going down, Sal? Who's the guy with balls bigger than brains?"

"You first, who's the broad?"

"My other investor."

He grinned and not in a friendly way. "I could get invested in her."

"What's happening Sal? Who put them down?"

When I used to deal with Sal, he was always on top of the game. Despite being a grass, he never looked afraid, never worried. But today was different. He was watching the passage constantly.

"No one knows, Clifton. They say there's a rogue squad moving about, settling old scores. Maybe from the company you keep. Been at all the parties."

Parties was an old word of Sal's. He used it to mean places where killings had taken place. But he had just said parties.

"There's been a few parties?" I asked.

"Rumour is it's your people."

Oh hell. I know where this is going.

"My people. Why the hell would my people be looking at this? And why would I come looking for you?"

"Who knows?" replies Sal, "Everyone has their reasons. Maybe somebody got fed up, up the food chain. Maybe army involved. Seems to be quick and lethal. Means we have to protect ourselves. Take pre-emptive action."

I can see Kyla's face, and she is panicked. I never thought Sal could come up with this line of thought.

"Sorry, Clifton, but self-preservation comes first."

One of the goons reaches forward and grabs Kyla by the hair, placing his weapon's muzzle to her cheek. Shit, this is going pear shaped and too damn quickly.

"It ain't my people, Sal." I'm shaking inside, but you can't show that fear to these types of criminal.

"Love to believe you, Clifton, but can't afford to take that chance, can I?"

I've never been a man who can shoot well. I'm a detective, not a vigilante, but right now I wish I was John Wayne. Damn, damn, damn. Think, dammit, think!

"Goodbye, Clifton."

"Can you see it on your chest?"

Sal's looking down at his chest and can see a small red dot. He's beginning to shake now. Which is good as I'm running out of calm exterior. Kyla's being a good girl, staying very calm and not doing anything daft.

"Lower the guns, Sal. Time for us all to walk away. Just lower the guns, and he'll drop the sights."

Sal continues to stare at this chest.

"You don't think I'd come here without any back-up. It'll be your funeral."

My knees are screaming at me to shake, but I need to hold the pose. Sal's now looking at me, and I stare right back, backing my hand to the hilt. And then I see his weapon lower slightly.

"All the way down, Sal. Everyone."

Sal nods to his men and slowly the guns go down. The red dot on Sal's chest lowers too.

"Good, Sal. Now my associate." Again Sal nods, but there's a bit of a fracas as the goon seems to be reluctant let Kyla go.

"Can smell you, bitch," grunts the goon. The man lets Kyla go, and she turns and drives her knee deep into his groin. It's a strike that could have broken a dam, and the goon doubles over and falls to the ground. Sal begins to raise his weapon but he sees a red dot on his chest again.

"Now, now, Sal. The man overstepped his mark. Let's just call that the lady's revenge."

Sal nods wisely. Dammit, Kyla, that bit of revenge nearly got us killed. But I'm still in the calm charade, and I nod at Kyla to leave. Slowly, we step away back through the ruined house, and Sal choses wisely not to follow. Kyla slides into the driver's seat and I tell her to drive.

"Where did that back-up come from?" asks Kyla. "That dirty bastard was all over me. Felt good breaking his balls."

But now she's staring at me. She can see my hands shaking, and the sweat pouring from my brow. And now she's beginning to shake too.

6

Chapter 6

"That was pretty dumb, kneeing him in the nuts like that."

She doesn't look up from her gin. It's almost as if she's ignoring me, but I'm going to push this point because it was really dumb. I don't care if he had his hands in places he shouldn't. We were on the way, clear of a bloody end, and she nearly blew that.

"I said it was dumb, Kyla."

"That was dumb? Never mind nearly walking us into a grave. Back alley, no back-up. I still don't know how we got out of there."

She's livid with me. And maybe she's got a point. First day in a new job and she almost gets finished off following her new partner. She's probably got due cause.

"That wasn't meant to go down like that."

"You're damn right it wasn't."

"No Kyla, you don't understand. I've had that snitch for twenty years. Been through all sorts of turf wars and that, and he's never been spooked like that. Never. He would have known who bumped off the Giradellis, there would have been word on the street. But if he didn't know, there's nothing. Worse than that if he's scared, he must reckon it's a major player."

"Or maybe us," says Kyla. "Maybe they all reckon we did it."

"Regardless, the knee to the groin was dumb."

She lifts her head and smiles.

"Maybe, but now they know you don't mess with this bitch."

I laugh and raise my beer glass. Kyla smiles, and some of the frost breaks down. I notice that she holds her glass between her thumb and forefinger only, almost rolling it between them as she drinks. The joys of being a cop, all the small irrelevant things we notice. It's why we are such bad partners. We see all the little minutiae that you have and just have to bring it to light. And we don't let you drive fast. But it's probably the long, crappy hours when you get down to it.

"So what's really going on, Partner?" she asks, looking intently at me. "I just got into town and it's turned into a powder keg, so tell me who's trying to set it off."

"Well forgive my pondering over the question, but if I'm honest, I'm stuffed."

"Really?" she says, the disappointment in her voice palatable.

"Really," I affirm. "Think about it. What do we actually have? A major crime family, so the people with motive can be found occupying many continents. A hot security system that stopped nothing. A crime scene with no evidence left behind. A grass who hasn't a clue when he normally knows everything. And an empty space waiting to be filled."

"Empty space? How do you mean?" She's staring at me with a look that speaks of worry. Maybe I have been too far ahead with my thoughts. There's things in my mind spinning around, and what I see in the days ahead worries me. There'll be death, guaranteed.

"There has to be a reaction. The Giradelli's will do some shaking down. People will be hurt, killed. But more than that, if this killer has a method that we can't track or stop, then there will be more murders and probably ramped up in frequency and number."

"Guess I picked a great time to join." Kyla has her head down now, and her long black hair is hanging onto the bar covering her face. It may be covering her face, but it allows me to stare without capture. She has such well defined shoulders.

"I think we should go to bed."

That takes me a little off guard and there's shock but also a leap of excitement from my heart before I grasp her proper meaning.

"You're right, we're bound to get a call soon."

"The empty space being filled. Good idea."

I leave a number of bills on the bar, and we head back to the car. The beer is having an effect as I keep sneaking some glances at Kyla as she drives. There's a thought about having a chauffeur in my head as she breaks the silence.

"Do you mind if I crash at yours tonight?"

"Mine, why?"

"It'll be easier when we get the call. You won't have to come pick me up as I don't know the city. We can be there quicker."

Well, it makes sense, but it's a bad idea. Not in a professional sense but in the "I've had a beer and my thoughts are somewhat relaxed sense."

"Sure. I don't have much mind. There's just a couch. But I can take that."

"Don't be stupid. I'm putting you out, I'll crash on the sofa."

We're driving towards my apartment which is in the Dillain part of town. It's not very salubrious, but everyone knows everyone in my high rise. Being a cop, and one that's reasonably well known, you need to live somewhere that people appreciate what you do and are prepared to back you up. So I'm surrounded by the salt of the earth. Persons from the fire department, hospitals, some priests and vicars, other decent working families. Anyone unusual about, and they soon let me know.

Kyla drives the car into the parking lot under my building, and I direct her to my spot. As I step out of the car there's a wave from James Cathcart, a fireman heading off on his nightshift. When he knows Kyla isn't looking, he raises his eyebrows in a male moment of congratulations. I shake my head and mouth the word partner. He simply mouths back "wow!"

We ride the elevator up to the fourteenth floor, and I lead the way to number 1406. Opening the door, I have to shove it hard, forgetting that I had left some trash behind it on my way out this morning. I let Kyla in and dispose of the trash in the chute at the end of the corridor. By the time I'm back, she's already found a blanket in my closet.

"It's very open plan," she notes.

"Yeah. Well, it means no one's hiding when I come in."

It's not a large flat, but it has what I need. There's a dart board on the back of the door, a small kitchen area, a couch with a television in front of it and a bed in the far corner. There's a small shower with a large extractor hood over it.

"Anywhere I can change?" asks Kyla.

"Sorry, no. I'll step outside."

"No, it's okay. I'll change with the lights out. Besides I ain't got anything to change into. My stuff's at the station."

I throw my jacket on the end of my bed and turn off all the lights. Despite my curiosity, I keep my back to Kyla as I change. Slipping under the covers, I realise she hasn't made a sound, and I look over to see she's still standing in the same position.

"What's wrong?"

"Have you got a toilet?"

"Eh, no. It's down the hall."

"That's unusual. But okay." Kyla walks out the front door and is gone about ten minutes. When she returns, I face the wall in my bed deliberately. As I'm lying there, it dawns on me that the calendar from last year is still on the wall. She's bound to have seen it. It was a charity thing and some of the girls downtown posed for it. There wasn't anything seedy about it, but they ain't wearing much. Miss March just happened to be the most exposed, and after the year was done, I didn't take it away. Hell, I'm a single male. And why am I apologising?

"Do you want some water?"

"Yeah, sure," I say, but I never take a glass to bed.

She stands over me in the dark, and I can see the outline of a glass. I take it in my hand and the lights from the train that disturbs this neighbourhood hourly flash across my apartment and also across Kyla. She just turns and heads back to the couch, swiftly getting under the covers. I really didn't need that image before I try to get to sleep.

7

Chapter 7

That's the damn telephone going off. You could wake the dead with that ringer. I guess that's the point as there's not a lot else which could wake me up.

"Detective, sorry to bother you, but the Chief wants you up and about."

"No problem, Sergeant." It's that DiAngelo, the female desk Sergeant. She's fifty years old, but you wouldn't guess it from the telephone. It's slightly Latin in tone but always so smooth. You could talk to this voice all day and never get bored no matter what the subject was. If it was any of the others, I probably would have sworn at them by now.

"It's not a problem, Maria. What's the trouble?"

"We got four dead in a single incident on the west side. Looks like retaliation. There's an execution downtown, some money guy from the Giradellis. And there's a knee capping down on fourth and Broad."

"It's kicking off then. Which one does he want us at?"

"None of them, Detective. He wants you down the Cathedral, the Anglican one in the city centre, St. Luke's."

"Why?" Despite the voice on the other end I struggle to hide my annoyance.

"There's been an incident. I can't say over the phone. He wants this on the quiet. I warn you though it's not pretty."

"Okay, Maria. Thanks. How's those kids of yours anyway?"

"Grown up and leaving me broke. University's not cheap."

"You're a hell of a Mom."

"Tell that to my daughter."

"Take care, Maria. Tell the Overlord I'm on the way." Poor woman. After her husband died, the eldest daughter hit any sort of drug she could get hold of. Maria got hold of her and got her cleaned up, but she won't talk to her Mom as the boyfriend got busted for ten years for selling the damn stuff. Who'd have kids?

I roll out of my bed just as Kyla flicks the table light on. I must look a pretty unglorious sight in my boxer shorts, and she politely turns looks the other way.

"I'm going to face the wall and get changed. Suggest you do too as we need to hurry."

"After those boxers, you're on. What's the call?"

"Murder, bloody murder everywhere, but we're heading to something worse."

"Worse?"

"Yeah, so bad Maria downtown wasn't allowed to say over the phone. At the cathedral. St. Luke's."

"Okay. I'm dressed, let's go!"

And she damn well is. Hair tied back, leather jacket and jeans with knee length boots but no real heel. White t-shirt underneath, holster showing slightly as she moves.

Meanwhile, I fall into some slacks and a shirt. Haul on the overcoat and brimmed hat, looking like someone on hard times. I hate it when the help shows you up.

***

St. Luke's has an enormous spire and is one of the main Anglican cathedrals in town. It's a hot bed for activists on welfare, homelessness, corruption in high places and any other real cause. None of the civic functions are held there since the bishop led the protests against the Mayor four years ago. Traditionally, it was one of the four large churches that covered off all the city's holier events, along with St. Benedict's, the other Anglican, and now favoured son, St. Brendan's, the Roman Catholic cathedral and St. John's, the orthodox cathedral.

I relate this potted history to Kyla as we speed through the city. On the radio there's reports of spats and fights all over the city, some deaths, all criminal gang related. But there's nothing on St. Luke's, which is unusual as you would get at least some benign traffic over the blower at least, even if everything was just about sorted.

There's only a few unmarked cars when we arrive, and I notice one of my least favourite crime scene experts, O'Halloran, waiting at the main entrance to the cathedral. Everything is incredibly quiet for a major incident, and I find it unnerving. The faces of the junior detectives are nervous, none of them looking us in the eye as we arrive.

"Is this normal? Normally uniform did the guarding of scene in my old place. These guys seem almost scared."

"No, it's not normal. And neither is that. Over there. That's the orthodox priest. His cathedral is miles away, what's he doing here?"

We exit the car, and I can see Tremmant, one of our guys from this district. He waves me over and takes us to

O'Halloran.

"What we got?" I ask.

"I ain't touched anything so careful where you stand," says O'Halloran defiantly.

"Okay. So what's happened? And why all the hush?"

"The Anglican priest, Father Domingo, is dead," announces Tremmant.

"So we have a dead priest," Kyla says. "Why all the strangeness? Don't your clergy die up here like everybody else?"

"Not like…this…Detective." Tremmant barely stammers these words out when he claps his hands to his face. He's trembling.

Normally, O'Halloran is all over me, pointing out the superiority of his scenes of crime team but he's positively stand-offish. There's a shake in his right hand. I have never seen him as much as flinch at a body. Last year there was the body in the river which made me puke, and he never moved. What the hell's inside?

"I'm not going in," says Tremmant, "But Father Krystanovic will accompany you."

"Why?" asks Kyla, clearly bothered about the strange ignorance of procedure.

"Cause he just damn well will, Detective," says Tremmant and walks away to light up a cigarette. When did he start smoking?

We walk over to the priest who looks extremely solemn. He's in his habit and is holding a cross in his hands. I tell him we should go inside, and he stops me with his hand. I don't speak their language, or languages, but he's blessing us and with a great intensity. I'm Catholic, and yes, I do believe, which means that I'm getting quite bothered by what's happening. I grab the priest's arm, and we turn to the cathedral doors.

They are large and wooden and take an effort to push open. The first thing I see in the gloom inside is the table in the welcome vestibule. All the hymn books and pamphlets are scattered all over the floor, but that's not what bothers me. It's the heavy sliver cross on the table.

The thing must weigh a small tonne if it's solid silver, and yet it's been turned upside down and driven into the table so that it stands in defiance to the Good Lord.

I cast a glance at Kyla, and she looks anxious. I bless myself and step into the gloom further. On the walls is what looks like graffiti. On closer examination, there are streams of words in different languages. I can only read the English, but they are a lesson in profanity and sacrilegious abuse.

"What do the other languages say, Father?" asks Kyla.

There are tears in his eyes.

"They are similar to the English, my child. Curses, profane statements against the Trinity. Some I cannot read, but it looks like the language of demons."

I try not to read too much, but instead walk to one of the entrances to the main cathedral body. Opening the door, I hear Kyla gasp over my shoulder, and she begins to break down and cry. I feel her grasp my shoulder and bury her head into my back. And I don't blame her.

The massive cathedral is a mass of graffiti like the entrance hall. Everywhere, in every nook and cranny all religious symbols have been upturned and abused into some profane image. And hanging down from the great roof of the cathedral suspended and swinging slowly is the abused body of a man. The damage to him is repugnant. But what really shakes me to the core is his face. It's Father Domingo, but not as I remember him from the television. His face is in terror as if he simply died from fright.

8

Chapter 8

It's morning, and I can hear the cross town traffic through the open window in the Chief's room. He's looking exhausted and a little overwhelmed. He's a touch overweight in recent years, but his mouth still packs a verbal punch, generally aimed in my direction. But right now he's holding his tongue due to the priest in the room. Father Krystanovic is sitting with a cup of water, also looking somewhat haggard. He has a large bushy black beard which the water has to fight its way past into his mouth. He looks like a damp woollen jumper.

Kyla's also in the room, but she seems to have a bee in her bonnet. Since we came back from the cathedral, she's been somewhat agitated. I've tried catching her eye but she constantly avoids my look. Maybe she ain't seen this sort of thing before. Mind you, she was fine with that head at the Giradelli's.

"You ever seen something like this before, Father?" asks the Chief.

"Not on this scale. But I will tell you this, Chief, this wasn't done by a man."

The priest turns his head to the window, and the Chief makes a swirly hand motion indicating just how nuts he thinks the Father is. Wait until he gets the forensic report, he'll go positively crackers.

"Well if you think of anything Father, then please do get in contact with us. Detective Trimble is the man you want. And thanks for coming down. It must have been quite a shock for you." The Chief is out from behind his desk and gripping the priest's hands.

"Of course. But be warned, Chief. There may be people behind this, but the presence that did it will not be caught by guns and handcuffs. You will require a different sort of enforcement."

"Indeed!" says the Chief in an act of blatant dismissal.

With the priest packaged out of the way, the Chief rounds on us.

"You two need to get a lid on this and fast. This sort of nonsense, especially in the current climate, could cause all sort of mad accusations and whisperings. Find me the person that did this."

"It may not be that easy," says Kyla, and I wince inside knowing the response that's coming.

"You bloody well make it easy, Toots! You ain't down here to make up the glamour numbers."

Kyla has her hands on her hips now, her arms pushing back her jacket, and her full figure is aimed at the Chief. As a professional, of course, I'd have to say her posture is impressive. She speaks before I can think any further.

"Toots? Glamour? Grow up, Chief."

Oh, that's a bad choice of words.

She continues, "If you had any wisdom, you would listen to the old man that's been in here. He said this was demonic."

"Oh for Pete's sake, you're not one of these weirdos too? Well listen up, sister, you need to hold that tongue and get that pretty ass out there and find me a killer. You do that, and you can hit me with all the theories you want."

And now he's turned his back. Just sat there, leaving Kyla flapping in her indignation. Better save her.

I take Kyla's arm and drag her out of the office before she says something she might regret. In fairness, she has every right to attack the backward, ignorant fool, but it doesn't do the job prospects any good. Better to wait until you have a few more wins under your belt.

I don't let her stop walking until we enter the lift.

"That sexist little prick!"

"Yes," I say and nod my head.

"Yes. Is that it? Thanks for the defence, partner."

"Wrong time, wrong place for anything like that. What's the matter?"

"What's the matter? He damn well basically called me a useless woman."

"No," I say. "You've probably been insulted before and called worse on the street. So what's the matter?"

She's facing the mirror in the lift now and avoiding my gaze. I press the emergency stop button.

"What are you doing?"

"Tell me what's up. Did the cathedral scare you?" Kyla looks at me with eyes of rage.

"I'm not some timid dame on a jolly."

"No, you're not. But you still haven't said what's the matter."

She lowers her head and shakes it slowly.

"I knew this would come out so you best know it now."

I wait quietly for her to talk more. She's looking for a response, but I choose to remain silent.

"The reason I was moved on from the other place was that I got "emotionally" involved. When I was in the cathedral, I could hear him."

"Who?" I remain aloof trying not to force anything onto her.

"The killer. The demon."

"I'm sorry…you hear demons?"

"Yes. I'm touched, as they say."

Well, this is a turn up for the books. Part of me wants to laugh, but another knows that I felt something dark in the cathedral. I reach forward and grab her shoulders pulling her close. Looking into the mirror, I stare at her face and try to be comforting, but it's probably a mess. Least she knows I tried.

"Good," I say, "think I might need a partner with connections in this one."

She raises her head and sees a smile on my face. She needs to be quick as they don't stay on there for long.

"I think it's time you got introduced to the best coffee house in town. We'll need to touch base with O'Halloran as well. Sometimes, you need a place to think."

9

Chapter 9

Espresso! I never put her down as an espresso girl but then what do I know. Not a lot about women, given my history. I thought the last one was just a pick me up. She's gazing out the window, playing with her hair but not in a flirtatious way. More nervous, distracted. I hear the whoosh of the steam frothing the milk that's destined for my latte, and a youth beside the till coughs politely. Was I really staring at her that long that he thought payment wasn't forthcoming?

"Here. It's a double shot. Thought you might need it."

"Thanks," she says and takes a delicate sip. Following her gaze to a man with a briefcase crossing the road, I see she's still elsewhere. Her jacket's off, and I catch myself tracing the line of her neck down to her curves. I bet there's talk about her back at station already.

"So what happened way back when?" I drag my mind back to the matter in hand and watch her turn to face me.

"One of the cases I worked on back in the old place, not the one with the kids, but it was about desecration in a graveyard.

There were stakeouts because the people buried there had money or rather their descendants did. But nothing was ever seen. But I could sense what was doing it."

"I'd have thought that an advantage," I propose as she breaks off for a moment.

"They didn't believe me until one night I dragged them down to the graveyard, and they stood there with me watching dirt dig itself up and a body drag itself away. There was a lot of panic when the report came in, and they forced the other guys to change their story, and I was put behind a desk for assessment. It didn't help that a goodly person, on the quiet, exorcised the spirit and so the practise stopped. To them, I was just a nut job." She bows her head and shakes it slightly.

"So you moved?"

"My fiancé didn't want someone from the funny farm. My parents were horrified and a lot of friends became very distant. But I knew what I saw and what I heard. When they saw I wouldn't change my statements about the incident a move was suggested. And it's followed me here."

"What? The same spirit?"

"No!" She lets out a puff of disgruntled air. "The ability. And the stigma will come too."

She looks up quite forlornly, and I try to smile, but there's an element of truth in this. Well, maybe a large breeze block rather than an element.

"We'll just have to find it, and show it for what it is. What is it you heard?"

"There's a hoarse whisper. And then a name. Like Darstone…Darstain…Barstain. The voice is very indistinct. But it's full of menace and loathing. And there's like a pressure. It's like a heavy blanket descending on my thoughts and shoulders, like a weight and not a pleasant one."

I usually am a man of an open mind, and after what I have seen recently, I am not inclined to dismiss anything that might help, but this is not going into any damn report. Either way, it's obviously touching her.

My phone vibrates in my pocket, and I make a grab for it just to break the heaviness of the conversation.

"Trimble, that you?"

"Yeah, it's me."

"O'Halloran here." Hell, like I didn't know. Even phoning the guy's voice is halfway up his own arse.

"What you got?"

"That's it, Trimble. I have nothing. A whole cathedral in ruin, a body that's broken in such strange ways, and then there is nothing. No finger prints, no pieces of clothing, no eyelashes, nothing."

"But the place should be full of stuff even if it's not the killers. It was an open cathedral."

"Exactly, but there's nothing. I spoke to Jenny Tatler and she said something similar. She found a few prints and skin, but they came from the first person to enter, otherwise nothing. She even checked that passage you found and again nothing. Given the violence perpetrated on the victim at the cathedral I would have expected to have found damage from fists and feet, giving some traces to the attacker…but there's nothing."

I place my hand over the phone and give Kyla a very quick precise of the conversation. Her eyebrows raised, she motions for me to return to the call.

"You spoke to the Chief?"

"Yes I have, and if he uses that language on me again I'll sue the bastard. Said that Tatler and myself didn't know what we were doing."

"Welcome to my world, O'Halloran."

"Did he say what he wanted next from you?"

"Apart from my resignation, you mean? Told me to get my ass back to the scene, but it's a waste of time. Tatler's been at this even longer than me, and whilst she lacks my seriousness,"–Hallelujah, I think–"she knows her stuff. We're both in agreement. Something got in and caused a significant injury and violence to person or person's without being harmed itself or leaving any marks. Oh, and I nearly forgot, as the Chief went potty at this statement–Most of the victims were dead before they were touched. Died from fright."

There are times in your career that make you think you are in the wrong job. Sometimes it's the pressure of work, sometimes the sheer ugliness of the job, and sometimes the damn management. Whatever it is, these times come. And this brief conversation with O'Halloran is one of those times.

"You there, Trimble?"

"Yeah, sorry, just processing."

"You need to speak to the Chief. He won't like it, but this is something special."

"You're right, O'Halloran. On both accounts."

Kyla watches me hang up, and I look into her eyes. I've had a number of years staring at people: victims, perpetrators, bystanders. The eyes tell a lot. In fact, sometimes they say everything you need to know. Unfortunately, someone's eyes are not admissible as evidence in a case, and you spend fruitless hours trying to find "real" proof. I need no proof here and now. Kyla is shit scared.

"What else does it say, Kyla? This voice, what else does it say?"

The saucer the espresso cup is sitting on vibrates at the touch of Kyla's hand. Across from us, the barista is working hard and making a clatter of a noise, but it's as if the rest of the world no longer matters. I thought it was the stigma of being different that made Kyla scared. The change to a new place and worrying it was still going to be the same old attitudes. But at the heart of it, it isn't about people or attitudes. It's that presence.

"Kyla," I say taking her hand. "I'm your partner, and we ain't been a team for long, but if we're to head into this together, I need to know what it is we're facing."

She looks away and there's no appreciative look from me at her figure. Instead, I reach for her face and turn her head back round to me. Windows to the soul, they say.

"Fènwa a ap vini."

"What the hell's that?"

"I heard it first, Mulgrew, back in the graveyard. I didn't think much of it, but after everything that happened and to check I wasn't insane, I went to a language specialist. It's Haitian Creole."

"And means what?"

"It's coming, Mulgrew. Maybe it's following me."

"What is? What is coming?"

"The Darkness. It's what it means. The Darkness is coming."

10

Chapter 10

On leaving the coffee house, I realise that if we're to go in front of the Chief with these ideas that maybe we need a little bit more back up than Kyla's say-so. After all, we have a killer that has left no signs, a voice in Kyla's head and a few Creole words. Not the easiest point to convince someone from.

Needing a little more background, I suggest that we should go and see Father Krystanovic as he seemed to be taking the same vein as ourselves. I try to ring the station in order to get his phone number, but Kyla spots him on a nearby television.

"There he is," she says, pointing into the window of an electrical shop. "Seems like he's on some sort of prayer demo."

"Whereabouts is it?"

"Just a moment," she says. "They haven't showed much background."

I come over to the television as Kyla won't have much of a clue about where things are from just pictures. The news program also seem reluctant to advise us but then again we can't hear the sound. There are tuts of a woman walking past, telling us to go buy our own under her breath. Cheeky bitch, this is police work.

"I got it," I tell Kyla as a tall building comes into view. It's the Sanderson Building downtown and also the tallest skyscraper. It houses all the people who ain't mere people in this town. If you own anything that's shaking the place, then your office is in the Sanderson.

It has its own private security, and not just the usual guys who patrol with their donuts and shout at us if it really kicks off. These guys are usually ex-forces or cops. Last year they took out a couple of thieves who were breaking in for certain company documents. Straight to the head and double tapped. Very professional. And all kept very quiet.

"Let's roll Kyla," I say to her, and she gives me a look that says I'm an idiot.

"Would you like me to roll across the car bonnet, and then dive in through the window? I'm right with you, Starsky!"

I give her a sharp look and then laugh. It would be quite nice actually, but I take the point. Where the hell did that come from? I must be more taken with her than I realise

We "roll" up a few blocks from the Sanderson as the traffic's a mess. No doubt it's the protest or whatever it is that's causing it. A couple of uniform see us and call us over. Apparently, there's an embargo on anyone else going to the building unless it's for work. I pull my badge, and the young officer steps aside with an apology.

"No need to apologise, you're just doing your job, and doing it correctly."

I used to hate apologising to a higher rank just for doing your job. Of course, I shouldn't have sworn at them either.

"Mulgrew, do we really want to interview him out here

in front of everyone? Best we take these sort of discussions inside."

"Good idea, Kyla. There's a coffee shop just opposite the Sanderson. It's pretentious and fairly crappy, but it'll do.

"Do you live on the stuff?"

I smile, but really, she's made a mistake there. You don't diss the coffee. Say what you will about me, but don't bad mouth the coffee. Can put a man off a girl that. Who am I kidding?

She's straight out into the crowd heading for the priest. It's a weird protest as there are no banners. I can see candles in what appears to be a mobile mass circling right round the Sanderson. There must be over two thousand people here, during the day too. But it's very peaceful. I see an old friend and tap his arm. Sergeant Houghton walked the beat with me and always has a moment.

"Hey, Trimble. Or is it Sir?"

"Come on, it's always Trimble. You're looking good Dave, how's the leg?" Dave was shot in the leg on patrol one night and since then has usually been at a desk. But he usually pushes himself out the door if it's a quiet job.

"Still gammy, still a pain. But still building the pension."

"Sweet man, what's the deal today? Looks like the best behaved protest ever."

"Well, it is. They ain't blocking anyone, and they ain't having a go. All they seem to do is walk round the place praying and occasionally reading stuff. It's screwing up the traffic, but after what happened to the priest, the Mayor is giving them a lot of latitude."

"You heard about the priest?"

"That he was murdered? Yes, common knowledge that, Trimble. Why, you know something different?"

He turns away when he sees my serious face. It's the stone wall he's become used to when my rank gives me privilege to things his doesn't.

"Who's the fox out by the priest there? She with you? You jammy swine. Damn, Janey would freak if I was working with her." He stares at Kyla and draws a breath. "She any good as a cop or is she just publicity?"

"Piss off, Dave! She's damn good. You're prehistoric like the Chief."

"Hey, tetchy. I know that defence. Best of luck. Looks a keeper to me."

"Enough, she's just a colleague. A good looking one but yes, a colleague. Anyway, I ain't got a sweet Janey like you. Worst thing I did moving up."

"Like you mean that. You just forgot to give the ladies that bit of special attention. Janey could have been on your arm. I was delighted the day you missed that date with her."

I laugh. She's a good woman but it wouldn't have been a good match. "Hey, I still get the odd cooked meal from her and that's good enough for me."

The crowd parts like the bow wave from a boat, and Kyla's there with the priest.

"Detective," says Dave, tipping his cap, and Kyla looks quite taken with his pleasantness. If only she heard him before. I wonder how they talk about us? Still, time to work.

"Good day, Father," I say. "Let's go somewhere quieter."

"Coffee! Better get used to that, Detective," says Dave, and I laugh again.

There's a crowd to get through to cross the street, and as they are such a gentle bunch with their prayer books and hymn sheets, I don't do my usual barging-through-a-mass routine.

As I reach the middle of the street, I hear a cry behind me. Turning, I see Kyla on her knees clutching her head.

"What's the matter?" I ask, reaching for her. But I am knocked aside by the priest and he begins to lay a hand on her and pray. Kyla's face is white, and she seems very shaken as the priest continues in his foreign tongue but with great strain. After a minute, he takes his hand off, and she gets to her feet, breathing heavily. I slip under her arm and help her across the street, the crowd breaking gently.

The coffee shop is there, and I force my way inside and place Kyla in the nearest seat shouting for water. A smartly dressed youth asks if that's "Still or carbonated?" and gets a glance of death from me. I give Kyla's face a gentle slap asking if she's okay as her face is so pale and vacant. Her eyes attune to me and then fixate.

"Over there. It's over there."

"What is, Kyla? What's wrong?"

"The Darkness. It's in the Sanderson."

11

Chapter 11

There was plenty of commotion for five minutes until I managed to get Kyla some water and get her to talk normally again. The priest was a great help with her whilst I sent everyone away. But now she's calm and rational again, sitting opposite of me with the priest beside her in this up market coffee shop.

"How do you mean it's over there?" I can think of no better way of phrasing it but it sounds like I don't believe her.

"It's there," says Kyla pointing at the Sanderson. "High up, near the top."

"Yes, it is," agrees the priest.

"Hang on. Do you hear it too?" I ask him.

"Feel. There is a presence."

"But she hears it."

The priest looks at Kyla and raises a hand murmuring a prayer. Staring at the Sanderson, she talks to me without ever turning to look.

"Do you think you can get some coffee?"

"Of course," I say, giving the priest a nod to look after Kyla.

"And Father, anything?"

"Just water, please."

"Still or carbonated," I ask, but the joke is lost on him.

"Whatever."

Retrieving a double shot of espresso, a latte and a still water with ice, I return to find Kyla and the priest in conversation. I'm usually the one who controls interviews, but I decide to let her take the lead.

"My child, what you have heard is not from this world. You called it the 'Darkness' but it is known by many names. I fear it was the darkness that killed my Anglican friend. We are here today to keep it trapped. This city is erupting with underworld killings, and the Darkness may have started those too."

"Trapping it?" asks Kyla. "How do you trap something like this?"

"We have surrounded it with prayer and blessing and have commanded it to stay. And so far it has. But it is too high up from us. And I fear at some point we will have to leave."

"Why is it talking to me?" asks Kyla. Her face is starting to show more colour but is still very pale. "Why me?"

"Some people are more attuned. Do you believe, my child? Do you believe in a Good and an Evil?"

"Yes," Kyla nodded vigorously.

"You should wear this," said the priest, "not for protection, but to remind you who you can turn to for protection." He laid his hand out and in there was a small silver crucifix on a chain in his palm.

"Thank you, Father, but there's no need." Kyla pulled her top down enough to expose the nape of her neck. With all the time I had stared at her neck I hadn't clocked the thin gold chain at the edge of her top. A small cross was hung on the chain, dangling now at the top of her chest. "I'm protestant though, Anglican."

"That's not important, child, only if you believe. It is the same God."

"Sorry to interrupt, Father," although I'm not really, "but getting back to the Darkness, what is it?"

"Detective, it is something abhorrent, but then you have seen that. It is totally evil and wanton in its destruction. But it is a thing that is controlled, to a point. Like all evil, it is only managed, never fully dominated, and therefore is extremely dangerous as it will turn the person who uses it to further and further evil."

"Okay, Father," I say, "but what is it? How is it a thing? And how does it move about killing people? And why is it here? And how do we stop it?"

The priest is staring at me. His eyes seem wild as if I have asked for a million bucks to pay for a sandwich. He bows his head and shakes it vigorously.

"No. No,no,no. You must not get involved. She cannot be brought close to this horror with her perceptions." He raises his head and looks directly at Kyla. "Child, stay well clear of this."

"I can't, Father," says Kyla. "It's my job."

"Hang on a minute," I interrupt, "let's hear the man out." I really don't want to put a woman with an unstable past into a similar sort of future. But Kyla's giving me daggers with her eyes.

"Mulgrew, I don't need protecting, and I ain't some mental case that needs help."

"I'm just saying we should hear the Father out before making hasty decisions. And irrational ones based on your history.

Dammit Kyla, you're too good to end up wasted on this nonsense."

But now she's in a mood with me. The arms have folded, and she's turned slightly away from me, her chin raised slightly in indignation. I could slap her and knock some sense into her. But that's not really advisable. Or wise. And, yes, I know, it's not what's done these days. Those old films were easier where you could just slap a dame talking nonsense and she'd come round and almost thank you for it. These days you have to get inside their heads and debate the point. Man wasn't designed for that.

"So, Father," I say reigniting the conversation. "How do we stop this thing?"

"You don't. Leave stopping the evil to us. Instead, find out who has called it. You need to stop them. Look for a rising star in all this. Someone called it here, and they wouldn't unless there was much to gain. It's too dangerous a force to simply click your fingers for."

"Okay, follow the money, follow the power. That I can do, and it should keep Detective Corstain here, from being too close to it."

"And Detective," says the priest. "Who owns the Sanderson building?"

"Why it's Grantham Holdings. George Arthur Grantham esquire, real estate mogul, probably owns about a quarter of the city. But the building is rented throughout by plenty of movers and shakers. It's like a who's who of the city."

"It wouldn't hide out in any old building, Detective. Someone is holding it up there. Someone up there is involved in this."

"You sure you couldn't get me a more prominent line-up Father, nearly every elected official is up there, except the current mayor. He refused and then went and took up residence in the Edelweiss district."

"Find who and find out quickly. We will try to restrict its movements, but it will not be easy. You see it needs to feed. I fear my friend, the Anglican priest was merely fodder for it."

Kyla is wide eyed. "Fodder! It did that to him for fun?"

"From loathing and hate. The Darkness, it is called that for it is without light."

"But Father, hell, it ripped.., shit."

"I know child. Detectives, find out who. I will return to my people and keep watch over the Sanderson. God be with you."

The priest rises, and I see Kyla look at me, fearful yet determined. We sit for a few moments in quiet, absorbing what the priest has said. If I hadn't seen the cathedral I probably wouldn't have believed most of what he said but.., well some things have to be seen to be believed.

My phone vibrates in my pocket, and I drag it out. The Chief. I show the picture to Kyla. It has a photo I took of him in a mood with the legend, "Bollocks what have I done now" written under it. She manages a smirk.

"Keep this between us at the moment, Kyla. Things are too weird to talk about openly."

"Made that mistake before," she replies.

I answer the phone.

"Of course, I'm on the case... Well, we all want answers, Chief..."

I really need to phrase things better when speaking to him.

12

Chapter 12

I'd really like to just go round the upper floors of the Sanderson, but considering the clout of the people living up there, you need to have a damn good reason for disturbing their privacy. And I ain't got a poor excuse, never mind a good one. So instead, I need to find a lower connection to those in high places.

Luckily, Kyla is more of a whizz on the computer than myself, and she's sitting at the laptop in the evening sun by the city's lake. There's one thing everyone says about me. and I take it as a compliment rather than a slur. If you want a copper to tell you where to go for coffee and doughnuts, then Trimble's your man. The doughnuts are a lie though. I prefer a Danish.

By my reckoning, if you are going to bring a demon, or whatever this Darkness is, into the world at risk to yourself, then the stakes need to be high. So who could the players be? I pose this question to Kyla.

"Well, given I don't know any names yet, I'll be generic," she says. The colours back in her face, and I'm glad I got her to drive us out to the lake. There's a quaint little coffee shop sat on its eastern edge where you can get some remarkably good blends. The young lad that generally works there knows me and my tastes for the black stuff and often brings new flavours to my attention. The place also has Wi-Fi. Well, some things are essential.

"Okay then, be generic."

"Well," says Kyla, touching her cross on the chain with one hand, "the underworld would normally be the place to start. Major family taken out leaving a power vacuum. But instead there's chaos as no one knows who actually wiped them out. That's not normal."

"No, I never seen an organisation that lives on intimidation not broadcast how good it is at it."

"Exactly."

"So, who would benefit from the chaos?" I watch her deep in thought. With her right hand she's rubbing the back of her ear, tilting her head to do it and exposing her neck to me, the hair still tied up. With her issues at the Sanderson, I found it easier to focus on the job and less on her, but I am quickly realising I am quite taken.

"If you wanted to bring someone down in high places, in a legal way…"

"Go on," I say. There's a red hue across her face from the last of the day's sunlight. If she had a pair of shades and a moquita then I could sell this place across the world.

"Then you need to remove the thing that keeps them in their place. What's your Mayor's big electing point?"

"Law and order, anti-corruption and building up the housing in the lower districts." If it were an advert, I'd have her hair down.

"Law and order? We seem to be struggling just recently."

Despite being honed in on the darkest aspect of the recent troubles, we were both aware of how stretched the force was with the outbreak of killings amongst the criminal fraternity. It hadn't reached a point where the general public were being inconvenienced but questions were being asked.

"Granted, but it's a blip at the moment. No one's questioning if the Mayor can handle it."

Kyla nodded. "Maybe it's about money. You said the Mayor was going to build up the lower districts. Housing?"

"Yes, there's a major overhaul of the whole area. New builds and shopping malls, some high-tech industry being brought in with a subsidy."

"So real estate is going to get a boost. Who hands out the contracts for all this building?"

"Mayor's office. And it's going to be a small fortune."

"Any of the names in the Sanderson to do with real estate?" Kyla's smiling now, pleased with her line of thought.

"I can think of a few but get hold of the resident's list and I'll cross check it for you." I stand behind her and watch Kyla's fingers fly over the keyboard.

"Dennis Halshaft?"

"Halshaft construction."

"Samuel Ravensbourne."

"RFT, major housing construction."

"Ruth Jurose."

This one has me beat. "Dunno that one." Kyla's fingers speed over the keys again bringing up another search engine.

"Well, she's the CEO of Dalmert, heavily into services supplies into sites."

There's at least another eight names in the building that have major connections to construction. It's something to go on, but it still is nothing. At least not enough to go up to the front door and knock loudly with.

"Let's call it a day, it's getting chilly." I pick up my long coat and pull it on.

Watching her stand and then untie her hair, I am surprised at how happy I am to see she just flings her jacket over her shoulder. She's left her holster in the car but her gun is tucked into her jeans. There's no room at my waist to fit a gun in, but hey, still the same waist size as twenty years ago. Just a floating gut over the top!

The night falls as we walk back to the car which is parked at the baseball stadium. It's not the largest stadium, seating some ten thousand, but it is pretty atmospheric. There's a crowd gathering now for the game tonight, and blue and green are the order of the days in terms of colour.

Kyla seems a lot happier as she strides slightly ahead of me, similar to how she has been pushing ahead on the investigation. Of course, I would have got there too but with a slightly slower hand on the keyboard.

"We should get you to a hotel tonight."

"Do you mind if I crash at yours again?" There's a surprise. Well, let's try and not sound too keen.

"Sure." Missed not too keen then. "Why" would have been better.

There's a broad smile coming over her face as she turns to face me before resuming her walk. Well that was a bit unexpected.

"Gun!"

There's shots. Lot's of shots. Same place though. One gun, I think, probably automatic.

Kyla is running hard to a position behind a concrete square

which houses a tree. I race to flank her behind a park bench. There's people running and screaming now. I can see at least three bodies on the ground. More gunfire. A security man in the act of pulling his weapon falls to the ground.

I glance towards Kyla. She's not there.

There's a young mother and child trying to run, and amongst the general chaos I can see a man holding an automatic weapon. He's turning it to the woman who has picked up her child. As he fires, I anticipate the horror of seeing the protective parent and her child being massacred. But they are knocked sideways by a young woman at full pelt.

All three fall behind a tree, and I see the man move towards them. I step up and call a warning before firing several times. I'm aiming for the head, but the man is hit in the shoulder and is knocked into the air, dropping his weapon. Fortunately, it merely bounces before lying to the ground.

I run and stand over the man with my weapon trained on him. He's foaming at the mouth writhing and kicking out. He shouts at me, angrily, wildly, almost spitting out the words. My boot to his face knocks him out, and I handcuff him.

But his words ring in my heard, terrifying me.

"I know she hears me."

13

Chapter 13

The whole place was a mess. They counted twelve dead, most killed in the initial burst of gunfire. The perpetrator woke up from my boot to the face just before he was taken into the back of a patrol car. The man was rabid, raging and frothing. His eyes were swinging wildly, and then with a sudden focus, looked directly at Kyla and then at me. Licking his lips at me, he was pushed into the car.

The Chief turned up not long afterwards, and once he had been briefed by one of the detectives from another precinct, he came over to talk to us.

"Heads up, Kyla, here comes your first pep talk."

Kyla looks up at the approaching Chief and sighs. She's a little shaken and thoughtful.

"What the hell's all this, Trimble?" he rages. "I thought you were going to get ahead of all this?"

I raise my head and just stare at him. If he's packing that attitude, he's getting nothing from me. After a curse to the air, he rounds on Kyla, his nostrils flaring.

"They say Trimble took him down, so what were you doing

Princess? Just checking your nails?"

I snap. I really snap. Usually I can take his full-of-bull jokes, but he's not dissing Kyla after what she just did.

"Piss off, Chief. Just piss right off."

"You watch that tongue Trimble!"

"And you watch your own, you dumb ass. That Princess just threw herself in the line of fire to save a family while your sweet hide was getting all dangerous over a mocha at the station. Say another word and I'll break your jaw."

"Easy Trimble, remember who's in charge around here." His eyes narrow as he stares at me.

"Are you here for the inspirational lecture or just to screw me over?" I could have been more reconciliatory.

There's an uneasy silence until Kyla breaks it.

"Anything on the perpetrator, Chief?" Her hair is tied back up and her jacket's on. After the take down, she helped work on a victim and her top is covered in blood.

"Low life punk from downtown. Been done numerous times for petty theft, armed robbery, GBH but nothing on this scale. Make sure you get this typed up for me."

"Typed up? I wanna question that guy."

"You can't. You shot him."

He's right about that. Damn. And Kyla's not been here long enough to work around being my partner. I need another tack.

"What about some more manpower to nail this stuff down?"

"Sure Trimble, which one of my one thousand standing-on-the-side-lines officers would you like to assist you? If you hadn't noticed, it's been kinda busy out there."

"I need some more people!"

"Okay, but it'll have to be gofers only. I need all my detectives on case. Take a few of the new plodders when you get back to the station. Tell the Sergeant I authorised it."

"Thanks. When's he being interviewed?"

"The perp? Probably in an hour."

"We'll be there." The Chief looks at me as if I have just told him I was mixing the acid with the base. "It's fine, just observing."

"And don't you forget it!" He turns to Kyla. "Well done, Corstain. Go get cleaned up."

I tell Kyla she can get changed at the station, but she points out that she hasn't any clothes there. Neither has she anything at my flat, but she suggests we go there.

I notice on the drive back how her hands vibrate on the wheel, a nervous twitch taking over. Offering to drive, I continue to observe her, and she's fighting to maintain a front. Once inside my flat, I offer to step outside as my shower's inside and fully observable. Instead, she asks for a change of top, and I set off to rummage in my drawers. Hearing the shower splash on, I try to avoid looking the direction of the shower but my libido gets the better of me. It's not a pretty sight as red blood drains off her front. Her eyes are closed and she rests against the shower wall. I turn away again feeling slightly ashamed.

I hear the shower stop, and I pick up a towel and walk with my hand shading my eyes from anything but the floor. There's the squeak of the shower door opening, and she takes the towel from my offering hand.

"It's okay, I'm decent."

The green towel is wrapped around her and she walks to the sofa and sits down. She quickly stands up and begins moving round the room. Her hands are shaking.

"What's up?" I ask.

"I heard him there. He teased me about the child and mother. He was right in my head."

I step up to her and embrace her. Her head rests on my shoulder, and I feel her begin to shudder.

"The things it says. It talked about…stuff that shouldn't happen to a child…or a woman."

Kyla's sobbing now. I can feel my shirt becoming wet at the shoulder.

"I'm scared…so scared. It's like…he knows me. Knows what I fear."

I lift her head and stare into the forlorn eyes. Then I gently kiss her head.

"Hey, partner, I'm here for you." It's a bit cheesy and maybe trite, but it's all I've got.

"We need to go," says Kyla, so I reach out and hold her again, hugging her tight. Then I break off and grab the T-shirt I found for her. Without any shame, she begins to dress, and I turn away.

"I'm done."

Turning back to Kyla, I see her in her jeans and my top, now knotted at her stomach. It certainly never looked so good on me. It becomes awkward as I realise it's obvious I'm staring, but she walks over and kisses my forehead.

"Thanks, partner. And thanks for not trying to take advantage."

Part of me feels good about myself. But a part regrets that nothing happened. Like every man, I put my decency down to a missed opportunity, and the guilt forms on me.

"You heard him too," says Kyla. "You look like you heard him."

"Yes, but it was the perp who spoke as him."

"Good," says Kyla.

"Good?"

"That means that guy has been touched in some way. Taken to perform a shocking obscenity. The Chief said he was a criminal. I think he was chosen."

"Okay," I say trying to sound helpful, "but how's that help us?"

"Well, someone possessed him. Someone singled him out. Therefore there'll be a connection. Mulgrew, they've given us a way in."

14

Chapter 14

That isn't the same man in the interview room. I distinctly remember his face and the hate that was all over it as he fired off those rounds at the woman and child Kyla bravely pushed aside. There's no rage in the eyes in that room. There's fear, confusion, and possibly panic, but there's no hate. It's like he's being accused of something he can't even remember, never mind having the starring role.

We're down in the dungeons of the main precinct of the city and the security is heavy. The mayor's office are screaming for a target, someone who they can attack and bring to task for the madness that seems to be affecting the city. Apparently the television and radio are calling for the Mayor's head for this latest tragedy. It's like a co-ordinated frenzy. At least that's what Kyla says. I don't read papers or watch the news. It doesn't do to fill my head with so called agendas.

The good news is that I have been able to sponge two uniforms to assist the investigation. Gonzales is a young lad, Mexican and pretty bright. Hughes is a tour de force former sergeant who got busted down to patrol because she went after a white lawyer who was heavily involved in rape cases—the act of, not the defence of. Hughes is coloured and the lawyer happens to be held up as a champion in this city. But dammit, she was right. She just couldn't prove it and paid the price.

Hughes is standing beside me, all six feet of her, bushy, black hair surrounding a taut ebony face. She's in her forties like me, and I remember her starting out. Got a lot of respect for her.

"What do you think?" I ask.

"Sir?"

"Drop the 'sir' bollocks, Meredith. Been too long to start that nonsense."

She laughs.

"Does that look like a killer to you, Hughes?"

Tilting her head, she tries to size up just what I am asking. "He had an automatic weapon, and you shot him. When did he stop being a killer?"

"Question is, when did he start?"

"Trimble?"

She's staring at me as if I've gone mad. And she probably should, but that's not going to stop me.

"Hughes, look at him." Hughes looks through the observation window, protected from the perpetrator's sight. "If he was just anyone and you hadn't a clue what he'd done, would you put him down as a murderer and a mass murderer at that?"

Her eyes narrow and she breathes deeply watching the interrogee's every move. The small door beside us clicks open, and Kyla walks in. I raise a hand to stop her from speaking.

"Trimble," says Hughes, "he's a thief, maybe a bit of GBH, but certainly no killer. Too panicked. Too afraid for someone who just grabbed a subbie and went shooting."

"Exactly! Get Gonzales and get into civvies. I want to know that guy's last movements. Who he talked to, where he was. Get me a history. And Hughes, we need this quick."

Hughes nods and leaves the little box room we are holed up in. Staring at the man in the room beyond the window, Kyla almost looks piteous of him. She supports herself with arms locked out on the small table in front of us.

"Didn't you tell her?" asks Kyla.

"Tell her what?"

"What you really think? That man in there was possessed."

"She needs to find that for herself. The last thing I need is to be taken to the funny farm until I can prove what's happening. But you're right, this is our lead in."

"Have you eaten? I could do with something."

"There's a diner close by. It's pretty rank really, but hey, at this hour of the morning I generally eat crap."

"You know how to get a girl onside. Let's go. I doubt they'll get much more from him."

Kyla's right. So far they have found out his name is Lewis Ashton and a low level criminal. Otherwise, he's saying very little. It's like someone has him by the throat.

We walk the two blocks to the diner and avoid the press outside by wearing some forensic team jackets. The scene dismantlers are renowned for their silence. It's started raining, and I'm glad I have my brimmed hat on. Kyla seems to be enjoying the water soaking into her hair, but then again, she has more than me.

The burger is an emulsified piece of cardboard stuffed in between two hard pieces of wood. And the cheese is plastic. But regardless, I eat it and the fries. As for the coffee, I didn't even entertain the idea. An empty plate sits opposite me, and

Kyla wipes the last drips of grease off her chin.

"So, do we get out into the field like Hughes?" asks Kyla.

"I'd love to, but I still need to type up this report about the shooting."

"I forgot about that. Mine's done."

"That's 'cause you use two hands and not fingers."

She starts to smile but then becomes incredibly tense. Flicking her head round, she stares out into the street. Her eyes are moving, like she's following someone but there's no one there.

"What's up, Kyla?"

But she's gone. Just ran from the diner. I drop a twenty and leg it after her. She's very good, almost got some forty paces ahead. I wonder what's up, but then I realise she's retracing our steps towards the precinct. There's a small number of newshounds outside the entrance, but Kyla knocks a couple flying as she races into the building. I have to hurdle one as he recovers, but I'm still on her tail…barely.

Inside it's easier to track her as the disturbance caused by a racing policewoman in a station leads to lots of pointing, showing me her route. But by now I know where she's headed. I careen into the small observation room and find Kyla turning to come back out.

"Ashton's not here! Where is he?"

The interview room is empty, and I spin around and look for one of the custody team. I see Palmer and scream at him for Ashton. He desperately points to the cells in this lower part of the precinct. The ones kept for special suspects.

Now I'm taking the lead, and I soon reach the custody sergeant's desk.

"Trimble, Special Investigations! I need to see Ashton!"

"Trimble? Oh, yes sir. Well done on taking him down…"

"Shut the hell up and open the door."

"Well, sir, as you are the officer who…"

"I know the rules, but I suspect he's in danger, now open the damn door."

It takes him a moment to weigh up my face as genuine, but when it clicks, I see the fear on his. After all, Ashton is his charge. He punches a code, and I hear the door locks click. There's an officer at the door too who the sergeant calls to let us through, but the young officer stands his ground barring our way. And he's right too.

Kyla drills the unfortunate but diligent officer with her right fist, and he tumbles straight down. She's through the door before me, and I desperately follow behind her. There's six cells in this particular lock up, three down each side. The first one is occupied by a coloured man who seems in shock. Opposite him is empty. I hear Kyla shriek as I pass the middle cells. Both occupied and both have a man lying on the ground with a ghostly white face.

The last two cells have had their bars ripped apart. Solid metal bars have been bent like wire and torn from their mountings. In one cell, an Asian man is on the floor with his neck clearly broken. But the other cell is in a mess. Ashton is still in his cell but now occupies it fully – every damn corner, all at once. Kyla vomits.

15

Chapter 15

"How did you know?"

Kyla is sitting on my desk, hunched over, and looks more than shaken. I have to admit my stomach is still doing somersaults from the sight we saw. Forensics will probably take days trying to sort it out.

At the moment, the whole situation is on lock-down, and we are not allowed to discuss it with anyone, even within the station. The Chief has taken personal command of the "clean-up" and I've been told to keep out of the way and get back to finding out what's been happening. It's a bit funny as the Chief isn't normally one to take charge but instead typically uses one of us plebs below.

"I asked how you knew."

It's taking a bit of time with Kyla to get her refocused. The whole image of the cell is no doubt rumbling around her mind, as it is in mine, but we need to get on to this quickly. So far it's been the Giradelli's, the priest, the people at the stadium and now our gunman and some criminals. Bet she's glad she transferred.

"I saw it."

"You saw it? Where?"

"Outside the diner. Didn't you see it? Black and brooding, snorting and with such a presence. And eyes that...full of hate."

"Kyla, I saw nothing. Not until the cells. And then just the blood bath."

"It was definitely the presence. The thing that has spoken to me before. And there were a number of symbols on it. We should get the sketch artist, and I'll tell him about them so we have some proper copies."

It's good that she's coming round to being a cop again instead of a shocked onlooker, but I'm not too happy about keeping this in house at the moment. The trouble with the sketch artists, and they are wonderful people, but they are at the bottom and don't normally know what the whole case involves. So when some big wig comes in and asks to see the drawings they ain't in a place to exercise some discretion.

"Look, I know someone, Kyla. We'll take this to him and then talk to the priest. Better play the cards close to our chest. If the Chief asks how you knew, then it's just a hunch that had you running."

She nods. I guess she's been through the mill before with people looking at you as some sort of freak. Even a beautiful freak is still a freak to people.

I place a call to Father Krystanovic and find that he's currently back in his own house. The march at The Sanderson was broken up on the grounds of safety by the Mayor as soon as night fell. This ill-advised move obviously let "it" out. I tell the priest we'll be over to see him just as soon as we have been to my sketch artist.

Twenty minutes later, I'm banging the door of a tattoo parlour downtown. With a look that says I'm insane, Kyla is hugging my long coat around her. It's the fresh hour of the morning, and the city has that quiet hum of people just becoming awake. People most certainly but obviously not the one's who do tattoos. Guess the trade's not great at this time of the morning. I hammer the door again.

"Get the f… oh, it's you."

The words are uttered by a man standing in an open dressing gown. His white boxer shorts need washing, and his string vest fails to hide a gut a whale would be proud of. Grease seems to have evicted half of his hair, and his face has a rubbery quality which accompanies his loose fatty jowls.

"Yeah, it's me! Inside and get a pad and pen."

"Okay," he says as I brush past him. Kyla follows me, and I know he's gawking as I hear, "Hello sister!"

Once through the door, I turn left into a tattoo parlour, go past the working chair and then enter a back room. The place is full of posters. Some are of wondrous creatures, some of men and women, others of symbols. Most of the humanoids wear little clothes and most are involved in some deviant activity. To be honest, I'm trying not to look at them as it tends to freak your mind.

The man who let us in is known to me as "Sketch". He has a real name on file, but I prefer this one as it reminds me of why I am acquainted with him. For all of his various oddities and bizarre tastes, he is one of the best artists I know. And often the people I deal with don't want to come down to the station to work with our artists, as they are worried they'll get lifted for some other job they've done.

There's a black sofa which Kyla sits down on. The room is

stifling, and Kyla gets back up to remove my coat.

"Okay, I have my stuff. Wow sister, you are one f…"

"Language, Sketch!"

"Well, I was going to say hot lady." Sketch watches me raise my eyebrows and gives a look of denial. He sits down beside Kyla, and I see him deliberately touch his knee with hers.

"Sketch," I say, "we have several drawings to do and some are a bit weird."

"Right place then, Trimble."

"Yeah, but they don't leave this room except with us. If they do, then you'll be spending time down at the communal cells with various parties that have a vested interest in your financial situation."

"I owe them nothing."

"Bull…" Just chinned him about ladies being present. "Nonsense. But you can take that debate up with them."

"Okay, no need to threaten me with this lovely creature here. I'll do it for her without any threats."

"Enough," interrupts Kyla. "This little lady is right in front of you, and I don't need protection or some poor attempts at frottage from Moby Dick's brother." I am laughing inside. "Now listen up and draw, mister, or I'll break your balls with my knee."

"Ooh!" says Sketch. "Always love a feisty girl."

The first sketch takes about twenty minutes and is the creature Kyla saw outside the diner. Generally there's a lot of black, a brooding in the general area of the face and some rough markings. I guess some things you just can't portray in a picture. Then Kyla starts to go through some of the symbols she saw on the creature.

There's some that resemble animals, although deformed or

changed in some way or other. There's some circles and stars. But then there's a pentagram with some letters written around its points. I say letters, but they ain't from any language I know. As he's drawing it, I see Sketch get excited. A thought runs through my mind about how I should chastise him for looking at my partner, but then I notice he isn't even looking at her anymore.

"What's up, Sketch?"

"This symbol, I've drawn it before."

"I'm sorry? When?"

"Had a few requests for it. Tattoos, not drawings. Wide range of people too, some you wouldn't expect to be in my parlour, although all are welcome."

"Names, Sketch, I need names now."

"You know, I don't do names in this place."

"Bullshit," says Kyla, shocking him with her tongue.

"No, Kyla, he doesn't," I correct her. "But here is another option. Any of these people happen to be a female with looks."

"Well, may be a few." Sketch is hanging his head low.

"Were these tattoos placed in less obvious places? The sort of places you would expect to be normally out of sight." I see Sketch begin to squirm.

"You dirty swine. You take pictures of the women?" Kyla smacks Sketch across the top of the head with her open hand.

"Just to have a record of the tattoo."

"No, you don't Sketch." My eyes are sweeping the back room for any wires. "They wouldn't have let you photograph this, if it is what I think it may be. Where's the video cam?"

Sketch looks at me, weighing up his options.

"I think it's time for some home movies, Kyla. Got any popcorn, Sketch?"

16

Chapter 16

You might think I will enjoy this particular task, being a man, but when it comes down to it, there is a certain vileness in being a voyeur. The other point is that I am actually more interested in the faces in front of me, faces that often are very obscured. It turns out that Sketch doesn't just have a cam watching the situation. There's also a remote control and mini screen so he can work it in between tattooing.

"Do you ever focus on their faces?" Kyla's really laying into Sketch about his activities. It's her first taste of him, but my palette is already beyond disgust with him. He's a low life alright, but as I have said before, the people I deal with rarely want to come to the station to describe anyone.

The other problem we are having, apart from Sketch's choice of camera angle and focus, is that often the recording has been cropped to the "good bits" as our perverted artist put it. Faces are not at a premium.

"Sketch, how do they describe the symbol to you?" My eyes are trained on his face looking for any wanton lie.

"They don't, never. It's always a printout on a piece of paper.

And the funny thing is they always burn it, telling me that they don't want anyone else to have the same tattoo."

"We need all the footage," says Kyla.

"No way sister, do you know how hard it was to get all this quality? It stays with me."

"Then it can accompany you down to the station. I'm sure the DA would love to…"

"Kyla, look! That woman there, back it up to her face. Do you recognise her?"

"How would I recognise her?" says Kyla, "I've only been her a few days."

"It's Mrs. Martina Darnell, wife of local councilman James Darnell, the main opposition to the Mayor."

"Seriously?"

I turn to Sketch. "How many of these tattoos have you done?" Sketch's eyes are on the screen before us watching Mrs. Darnell undressing for her tattoo.

"Man, she sure was nice."

"Sketch!" I say, slapping the back of his head, "Concentrate! How many of these tattoos have you done?"

Rubbing his heads he murmurs an answer. "Twenty-five at least."

"Any tattoo buddies completed any?" asks Kyla. Damn, that's a good point.

"Yeah, quite a few I think."

"Are they as perverted as you?" says Kyla.

"Hey, a man has needs."

"Let me rephrase the question, Sketch," I interrupt, "Do any of them have cameras?"

"Not that I'm aware of. I don't advertise the fact."

Kyla takes some names of Sketch's colleagues in the business, and I gather up his data. On the way out, I see Kyla rip down a poster of a women who is looking particularly uncomfortable in the position, a naked man is holding her. It's a small triumph but it puts a smile on her face. Given what we have seen recently, that's a win.

I get hold of Hughes on the mobile, and she reports that her investigations are still in the early stages. So she has nothing. I tell her of our find and task her to tail Mrs Darnell. It's at this point I realise I haven't slept, and it's now early afternoon. I tell Kyla we need to get some sleep, and she agrees. Driving back to the apartment I can see she's deep in thought. As for me, I'm just knackered and am like a zombie staring into space.

I don't even think about Kyla being in the room as I drop into my bed, stripped to my pants. Behind me I hear her climb into the bed and there's an arm that wraps itself around me. There's a touch of skin on my back but I'm so exhausted I just drop.

There's the blasted ring of my mobile. I have my calls filtered, and this one's sounding the priority ringtone so I know it's Hughes.

"What? What's the matter?"

"You need to come, right now. I have her tailed to one of the posh apartments past the wildlife park. Thing is, there's a load of other cars here too. I think somethings going down. I'm pulled off beyond layby thirty two in the trees. Meet me there."

"On my way, Hughes. Don't do anything until I get there," I insist.

"I know the drill."

With an effort, I swing my legs out of the bed and throw back the covers. Over my shoulder I see a flash of flesh as

Kyla sits up and stretches. Now that's a sight to wake a man up a dozen times. I don't know what this is as we only slept together. And I mean slept. I must be getting old to fall asleep when a woman gets into my bed.

"You okay?" I ask.

Kyla smiles. "Yeah. I'm good." Pulling a top over her head, she allows herself to then stretch and yawn before standing and pulling on her trousers. I don't know what this is, but I also don't have time for it. Like I said, I must be getting old.

There's silence in the car once I've briefed Kyla on what Hughes said. I'm preferring this to conversation as I'm feeling awkward. Nefarious activities and death currently seem more like home to me. But she is beautiful.

I tell Kyla to kill the lights as we pass by the wildlife park and find layby 32. Hughes is well hidden, but I know how to find someone in the dark.

"They moved out a few minutes ago from the house up the road. They also had a lot of cages with them but quite small, maybe big enough for a large chicken. And all of them were in habits like monks."

"Like monks?" asks Kyla.

"Yes, but completely black habits, hoods up. Freaked me out. Also I thought I could hear baby cries from the cages. Not screams but murmurings."

I walk to the trunk of the car and unzip a large hold-all. I sling a shotgun over my shoulder and hand a rifle to Kyla. She shakes her head and taps her own gun.

"I'm more accurate with this."

Hughes, however, takes a rifle. There's a grimness on Hughes' face, and I can guess what she's thinking. After what happened to the priest, I am also following an unpleasant track in my mind.

Judging by the trail, I would put the number of black monks at twenty to thirty, and Hughes says she counted twenty-four. Apparently, they all arrived in that garb, and she's struggled to catch a glimpse of any face.

The trail isn't too long, and we come across the gathered throng inside the wildlife park fence. They have cut a hole in the fence or rather recut a hole in the fence. The rear of the park is still not fully developed, and they have gathered in a rough hewn amphitheatre created by diggers shifting unwanted boulders around.

We're still at quite a distance, and Hughes takes some small binoculars hanging from her neck and begins to look more closely at the scene. A murmur starts up on the breeze, and I realise it's coming from the amphitheatre. I can't make out the words and there's no lights.

"Hughes, what's happening?"

"Hard to tell. I ain't got the NVGs. There's a central figure who seems to be holding some sort of blade, possible machete. The others are gathered round, chanting, singing, whatever that noise is. There are two other figures who are beside the cages close to the main person. I think they are opening one up."

There's a churning in my stomach and I pray to God that my hunch is wrong.

"Shit, Trimble, that's a child they've got."

If I could hit them with my shotgun from that distance I would have. Instead, I leave the women with their shock as I leap up and sprint hard. It's a descent down loose gravelly soil, but as I look up, I see the figure with the blade now holding a child by the ankle. There's no time. I cock the shotgun as I'm careering down the slope and fire.

17

Chapter 17

I don't have my feet firmly planted as I fire so I am knocked off balance. That combined with my precarious descent causes me to fall and begin to roll down the slope. There's a sound of a melee beginning and more gunshots. As I reach the bottom of the slope, I lift myself up as fast as I can and quickly spot the hooded figure with the blade. But I realise that my shotgun's been dropped on the slope. Crap, nothing else for it.

The poor child is held up by one ankle, and the figure has its other arm swept back in a motion that indicates a swing is coming. Despite the shots I fired, the hooded person is chanting and muttering in who knows what language. My ribs ache, and my head is spinning slightly as I run towards the figure and dive at the person just as they begin to swing the knife.

I make contact before the blade arrives. As the figure stands, I drive my head into its chest and fall over the child. From the corner of my right eye, I see the blade as his arm has swung across my back and wrapped around me. Driving my legs,

I lift us off the ground and push him hard until we descend again on the bare mucky earth.

The child is crying but is between us, and I quickly wrap the poor baby in my arms and try to roll away. But I only succeed in rolling into a foot which then kicks me in the back. Looking up, I can see a woman's face inside the cowl she wears. There's eyes full of anger and hate, wild like someone returned from the jungle after many years.

Then she lifts her face and says "kill him!"

Flicking my head round to the subject of her words, I see the hooded figure I had just tangled with, and he has the blade, and I can confirm now it is a machete, point down and about to be driven into me. I wrap the baby up as tight as I can and try to turn it away from the blade.

There's a loud crack of gunfire, and I see my assailant get whipped into the air, his shoulder having taken a bullet. The hooded woman cries out and begins to run. But the man stands up again, and with his good side comes at me again. This time he is shot in the temple and I cover my eyes as he falls away from me.

Then there is the sound of a shotgun and screaming children. I recognise Hughes standing over me, my shotgun in her hand and a rifle over her shoulder.

"Stay there, Trimble. I got your back."

"Go get them!" I shout. "We need to get them."

"We have a large number of unprotected children and these sick monks are scattering in all directions. We stay put, Mulgrew, and await back-up." I recognise Kyla's voice and there's a relief that she is alright. She's also correct with regards to our actions. But she didn't see the eyes of that woman. What sort of stuff are we digging up here? The priest was something else and it was a ghost or spirit or something, but this was a child they were about to lay waste to. A human child. And these were people.

"There's one dead, Trimble, the bastard that was going to kill the baby," says Hughes.

"Yeah," I groan, "thanks for that. I thought I was gone."

"Don't thank me, thank your partner. She's a better shot than I ever was."

"Hughes," Kyla says without acknowledging the compliment, "go check on the other children but don't let them all out until we get some help." Hughes' legs are replaced with Kyla's worried face.

"You okay?"

"Glorious," I reply above the cries of the child in my arms. Kyla reaches down and takes the child cradling the little one and gently singing to him. I roll up to my feet and remove my jacket, offering it to Kyla to wrap the child in. I watch enjoying this moment of human compassion after the horror show just witnessed. In the distance there are sirens.

"Don't recognise the dead one," says Hughes. I've known her for years and I have never seen her look so white. Her training is keeping her going, pushing back the reality of what we saw but there's a mother in there screaming and convulsing at what was about to happen. God, in case I forget this at confession, I owe you one for this. This couldn't have gone bad. It just couldn't.

***

An hour later and I'm sitting on the back steps of an ambulance having had a young paramedic give me the once over. He says I'm in shock, which to be fair a drunk would have spotted, but otherwise just some very heavy bruising

86

around my ribs.

There's now an entire circus of authorities at the park: police, ambulance, social services amongst a myriad of others. Apparently, there was an abduction from an orphanage. The staff there were knocked out and tied up, and it was only a passing patrol noticing no lights in the place that meant anything had been discovered before sunrise.

There's a Salvation Army coffee wagon on the perimeter of the scene. They usually turn up at major incidents to assist with the catering for hungry cops, fireman or any other rescuers. I'm not too sure what the coffee will be like, but at least it should be warm.

At the hatch is an elderly woman, maybe close to eighty, and I ask her for a coffee. She hands me a large paper cup of black tar, and I recognise instant in the cup. Still, it is hot. There's a bacon roll too, and inside I'm grateful. I look for somewhere to sit, and the woman must see my predicament as she tells me to come round the side of the wagon and use the access steps.

"You did well." Her voice is slightly croaky but strikes me as sincere.

"Thanks, love. And thanks for this," I say holding up the roll.

"Are you okay?"

I am about to give her the standard police response in the affirmative but her eyes stop. She's not just being kind or polite but rather she seems to really want to know. "No love, no I'm not. You don't see that sort of sh… sorry, stuff, everyday. Kinda freaks you out. You wouldn't think people could be so… well you know."

"Is there anything else you need? Anything I can help you with?"

"No love but thanks. What's your name?"

"Ethel."

"Detective Trimble. It's good to see a bit of decency after that."

There's tears in my eyes. Children, they were going to butcher children! Right there in a field. And do what with them? I break down and begin to sob.

Ethel has her arms around my head and is whispering quietly. I can hear her praying, earnestly. Praying for me, for the children, for the city. It's all I can do to manage an amen at the end.

I stand up and turn to thank her. She's still watching me intently.

"Thank you, Ethel."

"I'm always here for anyone. But especially for a brother."

"Actually I'm Catholic."

"That I didn't know. But I knew you were a brother." She smiles and turns away back into the coffee wagon. I raise my head to the sky and give a nod to the man upstairs. Then my eyes come back down to the mess before me. My shoulders feel heavy and tired. I am struggling to get my head around the things that are happening. But this is my city, and it's time to go clean it up again.

18

Chapter 18

We're back at the precinct because I need to get my head together about our next line of attack. There's been statements and all the usual procedures involved with a major incident, but to be truthful, I am somewhat distracted. There's times in my life when I have faced death but never have I seen such evil eyes. Mad eyes, wicked eyes and even cold eyes, but never such malice and malignance.

Kyla and Hughes are about somewhere, making sure the loose ends are tidied up. Apparently, the orphanage workers were in tears at the return of the children. Some of the uniforms Kyla spoke to said that the workers were pretty traumatised, and that social services were on-route with a whole team of shrinks and doctors. Apparently, the baby I had shielded was called Hope which makes me chuckle, especially when Hughes says I'm the last true knight of the city, protecting hope.

There's a rumour too that the Chief wants to stand me down due to the trauma from my recent experiences, but that's not going to happen. He spoke to Kyla who said she didn't know where I was. I know this because I was sitting behind her at the time. It actually bothers me, because it's not like him. Usually, he flogs you to death, and only when you can't think or move would he let you go home. And that's the thing, he only lets you go home, he never, ever, sends someone home.

I'm sitting at my desk on the third cup of coffee when a young officer I'm not acquainted with knocks on the door and jukes his head around before settling on myself, the only person in the room.

"Detective Trimble?"

"Yes, son, what is it?"

"They want you over at the psychiatric holding cells."

"Why?" I ask. I'm struggling to remember the last time I was at those particular cells. There's only two, and they are for people who struggle to control themselves. The padding's fun to jump into, according to the desk sergeant's children.

"There's a loonie over there mentioning something about the priest that died over at the Anglican cathedral."

I leap from my seat and brush right past the kid. Kyla's walking the other way with a stack of paperwork.

"Where you going?" she asks.

"The nut wing. Got a loonie who is talking about the priest murder. Join me when you get five."

She nods, and I hurry across the building and down the stairs to the second floor where the special cells are.

Normally there's a desk sergeant and another officer, as you have to book prisoners in and out, but since this is a quiet wing, they are often in the office at the side. But all I can see is the Chief at one of the cell doors.

"Trimble, about bloody time. Come and take a look at this

guy." The Chief has the viewing window snapped back and is waving me over. As he steps aside, I look into the cell and see a hulk of a man sitting in one corner. The brute must be at least seven foot, wide as a lorry and with wild, ragged, black hair. He's staring at the floor, occasionally snorting.

"What's the deal with him, Chief?"

I feel something push into my back and recognise the end of a revolver. The Chief's other hand reaches past my own and opens the cell door.

"Get in, Trimble. You couldn't keep your damn nose out of it all. If you'd have kept me in on what Hughes was doing, I'd have been able to keep you all out of this and none the wiser. Instead, I'm going to need to remove all of you. They don't like problems or issues. Have to keep your own involvement on track, clean up any of your own messes that get in the way or else he visits you."

"Who?" I ask, desperate to keep the Chief talking in the hope someone else appears. "Tell me, who visits?"

"Blacker than the night, with dreams and hells you cannot imagine. I have seen his work, Trimble, and I won't be one of his failures. Instead, I'll rise with him as the rest fall. But you're stalling. So get in there!"

"Wait..," but I am pushed into the cell.

"Pity, you were a half decent cop." And the door slams shut behind me.

Half decent, cheers. But then I remember there's someone in this cell. And he's stirring. Oh damn, he is at least seven feet tall.

There's one good side to his being so tall, and that's that he can't stand fully upright, unlike short arse me. However, this advantage of mine is somewhat outweighed by the tennis bats he has for hands and the biceps that Lou Ferrigno would be astonished at. I look around for a way out, but there's only the door and that's locked tight. Turning back, I stare into the brute's eyes and they seem empty. Or rather distant, as if he's not at home.

He lunges forward with his great hands, and I roll desperately to one side. But he's quick, and before I can get back to my feet, he's planted a boot into my side. Guys in here ain't meant to have boots. Nor is he meant to have a knuckle duster that he's drilled into my side. He picks me up and throws me across the room. The walls may be padded, but it's still damn well hurts, and I'm struggling to catch my breath.

With a desperate effort, I stand and swing the best right hook I have. His face didn't even move, and my hand feels like it punched a wall. He reaches out with his right hand and grabs me by the throat, pinning me to the wall, choking the life from me. I cough and splutter as I fight for breath and struggle to keep my mind thinking. I try to swing a kick to his nether regions but can't reach.

The door of the cell clicks open. Kyla races in and yells at the brute to stand down. He turns from me, still holding me in mid-air and tracks straight at Kyla. He swings, and she ducks before throwing three swift punches to his face. He's unmoved, but she seems equally unfazed. He swings again, and she steps away before running in close to him, swiftly kicking him hard between the legs. Again, he doesn't even flinch.

There's not much left in me as I dangle by the neck. I can't even raise my arms to help myself anymore, and there's a part of me that's starting to accept my fate. Dear God, this looks like it. Going home, as they say. And not in style. Then I see

Kyla move inside his swinging arm again and grab his wrist. She seems to run up his chest and leap back over his arm twisting it violently. There's a loud crack, and his grip on me is released. I can't even reach out to break my fall, I just crash down onto the, thankfully, padded floor.

There's some more violent strikes I hear before footsteps entering the cell and then die out abruptly on the padding.

"Get back Corstain, I've got him." It's Hughes, and I look up to see her holding a shotgun. It's pointed at the brute that nearly killed me. Kyla is standing in front of him and has blood across her face. She's sweating profusely and is focused on the cell's occupant. He then turns his face to me, and I see his eyes again. But this time they're not vacant, not dispassionate. There's a fear there, a terror and an incomprehension. He begins to shriek and swing out with his good arm. Kyla leaps back and Hughes points her weapon at his head.

"Everyone back. Time to take this madman down," shouts Hughes.

"No!" I yell. "No! Everyone out. Everyone out of the cell." They look in surprise at me but the wildfire in my eyes convinces them. "Leave the door open and have that shotgun primed, Hughes." The last bit is delivered in a croak as I'm still getting my breath back.

Everyone stands outside the cell, and the brute looks carefully at the door and then at me on the floor. He briefly steps towards me, causing shouts from outside the cell, which I wave down. I hope I have this right as he draws near. Standing over me, he passes a hand over my shoulder and head. Abruptly, he then pulls away to a corner of the cell where he sits on his knees. His head bows and he begins to sob.

Slowly, I get to my feet and walk to my former abuser and

lay a hand on his shoulder. Poor used kid. Turning round, I exit the cell and groggily look for Hughes. There's maybe two of her or she may have someone with her, but I don't really care.

"Hughes, he needs some medical attention and someone who knows how to deal with his mental condition. In fact check the mental institutions as I think he may be missing. Don't harm him, he's just been messed with." I look back and there's pity in me for him. But there's also a rage at the man who did this.

"You need some medical attention yourself," says Kyla, smiling through the blood across her face.

"Have to wait. Where's the damn Chief?"

19

Chapter 19

There's a deputy station commander from a cross town coming over to take over the running of the precinct. This is due to the scene I'm looking at in front of me. The Chief's large desk, which he liked to sit behind whilst telling me I was useless, is still full of the paper and stationery that it always held, but now that everyday part of police life is covered by another too often seen part of our work—blood. And more than blood…but there's no need to be gross about what's in front of me.

The Chief's body is in his seat, a shotgun on the floor, and as you can imagine, a lot of mess. I'm feeling a little numb. Well, that's a lie. I'm freaked by this turn of events, but as the senior officer on my small team, I'm giving the impression of calmness and responsibility. Professionalism as it's finest. Thinking these things is stopping me from wondering why this grumpy genius of a detective tried to have me killed and then blew himself to bits.

And those eyes. The same darkness that was in the hooded woman's eyes at the zoo was present in the mentally challenged hulk in the cell. He went for treatment, and then was taken back to his institution. Poor guy has never gotten above a mental age of five, and he gets to see all that.

I take a walk to the canteen downstairs, which has got the full canteen staff looking a little shocked as they make the breakfasts. Word is hovering around the station as to what happened, and I know I can't interject to deflect rumours. But then, what is really happening? I spot Kyla at a table with Hughes. Like myself they both look pretty rough, but I see Hughes has managed to force down a full breakfast. She always could. Kyla's got a small bowl of muesli. That needs to change.

"You look better with the blood off your face," I tell Kyla.

"You don't," laughs Hughes

"Are you okay?" asks Kyla.

"No. But there's no time to sort that out right now. Guess I was lucky you cleared that paperwork and came over."

"You weren't lucky," says Kyla shaking her head. "I felt it in the building. I grabbed Hughes and followed you to the cell."

"What the hell's going on, Trimble?" asks Hughes. "I nearly blew away a guy with the mental age of a five year old. We witness an attempt at child sacrifice. I have kids in this city. What's happening?"

I'm distant as she talks, lost in my own horrors. There's a television on the wall showing pictures of protests around the city hall, and the Mayor is seen under pressure from questioning reporters. And then there's another face calling for the Mayor to go, calling for people to make a stand.

It's very hard to get a reasonable idea from the television what's happening politically. There's too many banners and flashing words. They don't ever hold up the name of the person being interviewed on the screen for long. I hate television anyway. Give me an old movie, something with a bit of plot and decent acting. I don't care if it looks like it was written for the stage and not the screen.

I turn away and seek some coffee from the main hatch, but Hughes yells at me, "You gotta see this, Trimble." There's very little I "gotta see" in this life, except the snow and ice melting around a waterfall in Canada in early April. It really is something, you know, the framed water falling in the most stunning picture. All free and all naturally made. Amazing.

"What is it, Hughes?" That came out very tired sounding. I really do need some more sleep.

"The Mayor. He's resigned."

"What?" I ask.

"The Mayor. He's stepping down. Effective immediately."

I walk up to the screen on the wall and decipher the bright bars of white writing on red. It's true. Immediate. Stress became too much, city is out of control. Persuaded to let someone take up the fight, someone with a more robust response. Oh hell.

I see Kyla reading my face. It's been a sharp blast into our politics, and it's a wonder she is able to comprehend any of the names flashing across the screen. I must be showing more worry than I want to as I can see her face mold into a frown. Why is it that women can still look beautiful with a scowl or frown on their face? A man just looks mean, but not a woman. Kyla's no exception.

"They're saying there will be a right skirmish over who will take over," says Hughes.

"No. There won't be." I'm staring at the screen, and I can see a man in the background who I am sure the whole city will be hearing more of. And he's up to his neck in it. We've already implicated his wife in the child sacrifice incident. There's no way I am going to let that man take charge.

"He's not the main concern." It's Kyla and the comment is directed at me. "There's a thing out there that waltzes into rooms and slaughters people. That's the first priority."

She's right. And if we get obsessed with the mayor, we will miss the bigger issue. We need to close this group down and get their prime evil out of the city, back into whatever box it came from.

"Kyla, get hold of the priest, we need to talk and set up some sort of game plan. If my reckoning is right, the wilder incidents around the city will fade away. Someone will take over the criminal ranks and there will be these hooded monks throughout our government and services. We need to go about this the right way, because if they see us coming, then that thing will come for us."

I had hoped this would be a sort of rallying call to the team but instead they seem dejected and not a little fearful. The woman's eyes come back into my mind, and I realise there's plenty of reasons to be fearful. But that's no excuse.

"Hey come on guys," I say. "Have a little faith."

20

Chapter 20

The story about the Chief has broke all over the city's networks. Currently there's talk about stress causing him to blow his brains out, and the current unrest is blamed for it all. All very convenient.

The priest asked to meet us under cover of darkness and away from his cathedral. He's organising a large mass of people so that once the killing spirit is found, it can be contained. I have no idea how that all works but I pray he does, although he did say previously there may be some sort of counter actions required.

As we will have to wait for the priest, I decide to follow up on the governor's wife who was at the child abduction. Uniform had run checks to find her, but she wasn't in any of the usual haunts. Time to go to the governor himself.

His office is downtown, and having sent Hughes home for some rest, Kyla and myself come a knocking. The building is around the corner from the Saunderson and looks incredibly modern. There's glass everywhere and everyone walking about is well dressed in a suit or blouse and skirt.

The blonde girl at the front desk has one of those ear pieces on, and as I go to ask a question, puts her finger up and then indicates that we should sit in the nearby seats. Well, I ain't taking that kind of crap from no one. I don't care what technology we have, people can damn well speak to one another. I pull my badge. Ah, some attention.

"Apologies for disturbing you, but it's Detectives Trimble and Corstain, we'd like a word with the governor."

She smiles politely. "I'm sorry, detective, but the governor is all booked up this week, but I can make an appointment for next week if that suits you. Shall I say Tuesday?"

"No, you shan't. What floor is he?"

"I'm sorry, sir, but he's unavailable."

"But he's here?" I give her my best stare which isn't all that frightening, but it does cause a slip.

"Yes, sir, but he's unavailable."

I snort. "Well, he'll damn well make himself available." With that, I turn and head towards the stairs. I see the suits move towards me. Now, this is starting to get interesting.

"I am Detective Trimble in pursuit of a suspect whom I believe to be upstairs, and I ask you to step aside." At least they won't pull any guns now I've declared myself in a public place. But there's four of them in front of the stairs. I'm not sure I can make a dash around them. Certainly both of us won't make it. There's a brush on my shoulder, and Kyla steps in front of me.

"Step aside, gentlemen," says Kyla in a tone that defies them to disobey. "This is police business, we're in pursuit of a suspect. There's no need for any unpleasantness. We just need a few words with those upstairs."

The men ain't moving. Damn. Well this is going to get

unpleasant. I reach down inside my coat and grab a night stick. Just for defence of course.

The first man steps forward to grab Kyla, and she catches his arm twisting it up behind his back before throwing him to the ground. The next few moments are a blur as Kyla takes on all four of the smartly dressed guards, sending them tumbling one by one to the floor. Interestingly, she never attacks them, but merely waits for them to reach for her.

"What are you waiting for? Go!" she shouts at me.

Some people have grace and dexterity, but I am not some people. My running style is effective but not pretty. I begin to leap up the stairs, taking two at a time. It's the central staircase, and I can hear running footsteps from above. There's a landing to the left and I take it at full pelt to find elevators. There's a couple just entered, and I barge in beside them.

"Top floor, please!"

The couple look at this sweating man in a long coat who is sucking in air like it's going out of fashion. They press the top floor key but also the tenth floor as well. There's uncomfortable silence as we look at each other.

"Sorry," I say, "in a bit of a rush. You married?" They shake their heads. "You look like you should be. Perfect fit for each other, especially the way you were looking at each other when I entered." I see their faces change, the man being frightened and the woman soaking up the comments. "Oh sorry. Didn't realise you were having an affair. You really need to work harder to keep it quiet." The shock on their faces is priceless.

There's a ding. The doors open, and I let the couple flee the elevator. There's no suits jumping them, so I follow them out, which causes the couple to break into a run away from me.

I take the opposite corridor and head as far away from the

elevators as I can get. Eventually, I get to the rear of the building and find a service elevator. Pressing the button, I wait for the car to arrive, constantly surveying the corridor behind me.

There's a ding, and I look through the little viewing window, seeing no one inside. With two hands, I open the door and it's only halfway through the process I spot the man in the suit crouched on the floor. Crap. He has a radio which he grabs to speak but my nightstick has hit him in the face causing him to drop the radio.

"Stand aside and this will go easy," I bark at him. He drops the jacket, and I see the fruit of his hours in the gym. The muscles ripple across his body. Now I could pull my gun, but I'm never going to use it. After all, the guy's only doing his job, and whilst we can blag the pursuit aspect in the middle of all the current madness, shooting an unarmed guard won't go down very well.

He breaks into a quick run and reaches straight at me like a wrestler. I let him grab my shoulders pulling me close. And then drive my knee with all my might into his groin. Not once but three times. His hands come away from me and I drill his chin with a two handed uppercut. Hey, I fight dirty, it's why I'm alive to this day.

He's not quite out cold, but it's close. I drag him by his feet outside the elevator and then press for the highest floor. It's one below the highest marked in the other elevator. Damn. I'll need to hunt the stairs to go up.

The elevator stops, and I have my breath back. The door opens, and I'm relieved to see it's just a house cleaner with a large wheeled tub of laundry. I nod an acknowledgement and race past her. This floor is organised differently from the other floors. As I exit the short corridor, I find myself in a kitchen. There's a suit outside the far door, not searching but on an alert look out. There's a Chinese man in the kitchen, chopping vegetables, and he looks up. I flash my badge at him.

"Stay calm, sir, I'm just in pursuit of someone. If you can just keep working. What's your name?"

He looks at me and shrugs his shoulders. There's then a short exchange of what I believe to be mandarin. Oh well, this is going to be awkward. I'd rather not go through the other door and take on another suit, but the options are looking slim. Glancing round the kitchen for possible distractions, I see a dumb waiter with the legend "private suite" beside it. It's not massive, but I should be able to get in.

I wave the Chinese man over to me and try to indicate my intentions. There are blank pages and then there's this poor guy. Obviously, my communication skills are lacking somewhat. There's nothing for it, and I climb into the device and then turn to look at him. I point upwards with my finger. He smiles and nods, and with a shake of a disbelieving head reaches forward and presses something on the wall. A door slides down in front of my face, and I begin to ascend.

There's a short time of darkness before light floods into my captive cell. I see carpet, luxurious carpet, and then the back of a leather chair. There's a large table in the room which is adorned with paintings and quality wallpaper. Behind it is seated a man with a charismatic face who is signing various papers. The dumb waiter stops moving and there's a bing sound. The man doesn't move for a moment and then walks over to the dumb waiter. The front has a grill across it which I guess hides me and I have my coat up around my ears. He throws up the door, and I move forward from the cramped space.

"Ah, Governor, how are you, sir?"

21

Chapter 21

"Who the blazes are you?"

Well, it's not the worst welcome I have ever received. "Detective Trimble, sir. How do you do?" Always best to be unbearably polite to someone in power.

"Do you mind telling me why you are arriving in such ludicrous style? And this had better be a good explanation because right now I have a good mind to call your Chief and bust your hide back down to a uniform."

These people always think they have a right to order everyone's lives. "You could call him, sir, except that he blew his brains out this morning after attempting to kill me, and using a mentally handicapped person to do it." There's shock in his eyes. "Where's your wife, sir? I traced her to a satanic meeting where I only just managed to stop them from sacrificing some thirty children. Where is she?"

There's fear now on his face. And confusion. The cheery youthful expression is now a face full of horror and questions.

"Satanic? Child sacrifice? No. Not Sandy. She wouldn't. She's a powerful woman, but not that."

"Where is she? Tell me where she is, sir."

"I haven't seen her since two days ago. I have been busy with everything going on. Getting calls, requests to take over the city. All the problems at the moment, rumours of the Mayor standing down, had to be ready."

He sits down. Actually, he more sort of falls down. This seems to be a shock to him. I'm pretty good at spotting the actor, and he doesn't seem to be one.

"Have you spoken to her, sir? On the phone, or by computer?"

"No." He shakes his head wildly. "God, where is she? Satanic?"

"I believe so. I was too busy defending the children to ask them properly."

His phone rings, and he just sits there. It's important that if she calls he maintains a normality so that we can get to her before she runs.

"Answer that please, sir. If it's your wife, then I'd appreciate a normal tone and ask her to come and see you."

"What? A normal tone? How can I give a normal tone? Anyway, that's downstairs."

I suddenly think of Kyla. "Can you get it anyway?"

He glares at me but then reaches over and picks up the rather dapper phone. It's old style but with the dialler replaced by buttons.

"Hello? What? When? No... No, no, no." He slams the phone down.

"What was that?" He says nothing. "I said what was that?"

"She's dead. My wife is dead."

"How? When?"

"At the house...hanged...maid found her... Dammit, she's

dead!"

"My condolences, sir. This must be a heck of a shock."

"Of course it bloody is!"

I stand in silence, giving the man a few moments to take in what has happened. But I am also observing. He really does look broken. His head is slumped, and he has that shuddering motion that crying produces. Well, the sort that just thunders through you, unembarrassed and wild. Raw pain. If I give it time he'll fil the space, the silence as he becomes aware of his demeanour to an outsider.

"Sorry, Detective."

"No need, sir. Must have been a close marriage." I feel heartless, but hey, this is my job, and she was attending a child sacrifice. My sympathy has waned.

"She made me, Detective," he sniffs. "Without Amelia, I wouldn't be in the position I am today. She brought me this far. She held me through all the challenges of a political life. She…"

The door of the room bursts open, and in walks a figure I know but am not that familiar with as I only ever get to deal with her minions. Juliet Sambrusco is the city's DA and eternal friend of the rich.

"My dear Richard, how dreadful, I only just heard and came straight over. You poor man, what a shock, and with everything else going on. And who is this?"

I try to stand appropriately but can't think what an appropriate stance would be. So I slouch in my usual fashion. Either way, she's going to tell me to piss off.

"Detective Trimble, Madam D.A. I was tracing down the deceased."

"Well, Detective, looks like you are in the wrong place."

"Maybe so. But I'm not always so unlucky. I'll be back, Governor. And again my condolences."

"Take your time, Detective. And keep me informed," says the D.A.

Fat chance. She's probably up to her neck in this. Okay, that's a little harsh, but she'll be taken in by them. That's the trouble at the moment. Everything is wound up so tight, I can't prise anything open, and if I do try, then it gets firmly slammed back down. Hanged? Well, it was no damn suicide.

I take the elevator back down to the ground floor. On opening, I see Kyla surrounded by most of the security in suits. Her weapon is on the ground and has the chamber with the rounds separated on the floor. The whole situation seems pretty heated, but Kyla's unharmed by the looks of it. Unlike some of the suits who appear to be nursing banged up arms and legs and a few broken egos.

I walk straight past. "Corstain, come on, we're going." I walk on but hear the suits move as she tries to follow. There's a large gentleman who seems to be directing the rest. He's at least six foot four and a monster compared to me. Also in better shape. Oh well.

"You! Yes I said you! Why are you impeding a police investigation? What are you covering, brother? Shift it now."

He raises himself up. "Your colleague attacked my men, unprovoked. And..."

I drive my finger into his chest. Damn that was sore. "Look idiot, we were pursuing a declared fugitive, announced to your guys, who then attacked us. Now drop it or I'll get the uniforms down here to haul your asses out through that front door. And I'll make sure everyone damn well knows whose fault it was and that their security got beat up by a woman.

Now, your choice. I said move!"

I turn and walk away. Part of the trick is to act like you just expect things to happen. I can hear the shuffles and the heavy breathing as he thinks about this. I just keep walking. In truth, if we get bogged down into the legalities of what we were doing, even despite the current unrest, there would be some not so pleasant days ahead. But he won't want trouble either. The sound of Kyla's clip being driven back into her gun and then her boots clipping across the floor tell me I've judged this right.

"You were winging that," says Kyla.

"Shush, don't tell everyone."

"Did you see her?"

I shake my head. "She's dead. But not here. Hung at their apartment. I'll fill you in."

22

Chapter 22

There was a large team of detectives at the mansion house of the governor. Most of the top brass were about too from the force which is quite an indictment when you think of the piss-poor turnout for the priest. I was half expecting the same sort of bloody mess at the scene, but this was a straight forward hanging. But they were damn careful.

All the security CCTV had been wiped, and they had left no evidence whatsoever. Well, nothing that could incriminate anyway. Kyla did a lot of the footwork, asking questions of the various uniforms that had been involved, but it all seemed a dead end. I had just "stood and stared" as she had put it. "Thinking" is how I put it. Planning was actually more accurate.

It's now nightfall, and we're sitting in my favourite coffee shop. There's been something brewing in my mind, and I need to check with Kyla if she's up for it. I'm going to need the priest's help too, so we are awaiting his arrival.

"Been thinking, Kyla. It's time to go on the offensive.

So far we've been bounced around and tracks are being covered before we can react. There's something going on, a group controlling this evil, this force. They could have just eliminated the governor's wife like the priest, but instead they're using a cold, professional kill. All tidy. And we have nothing anymore."

She grabs her loose hair and bunches it into a pony-tail. With a practiced hand, she places a hair tie around it and then fans out the tail. I can't decide if this is for me or if my vanity is getting the better of me. I must be tired because my thoughts are struggling to stay on the job.

"Mulgrew, that's fine by me, but what do we have to go on? A women with serious eyes who you might recognise again. Everything else has been closed down." Her eyes are sad, knowing she hasn't anything to offer.

"We have a location. The Saunderson building."

"But the darkness is no longer there." She looks confused.

"No, but the people that called it are. We have a loose connection that the people in that building have something to do with the darkness. I know it's not a great lead, but it's all we got, and things keep moving on and people keep dying." I stare at her hoping to show I'm resolute in this idea.

Kyla laughs a little. "You know we are operating beyond what is legal?"

"I'm thinking this isn't police work anymore."

"Proper boy scout ain't you. You know we could just call it quits and leave for another place. Set up shop as investigators or something, get out of this dark city."

And there's temptation, sitting right in front of me. There's a song in my head, and I can't place where it's from. A song about women. Blessing and temptation all in one. She's got that look, and I know it's not my ego this time. I wonder if it's the closeness of the work that causes a nearness of heart. Her hand is touching mine.

I've been in this city for years, over twenty, and there ain't no other place that's home. And now someone isn't simply messing it up, someone is bringing something into it that is beyond criminality. And this is my city.

"We need to clean house first," I tell her. "When it's gone, you can take me anywhere you want."

There's a forced smile, but she nods in acceptance. She can't leave this either.

"The Saunderson," she says. "How do we get in there?"

"With difficulty, and we're taking a priest with us."

Kyla raises her eyebrows and makes to say something but the door of the shop opens and the priest walks in.

"Father," I acknowledge, standing and shaking hands with him. "How goes it from your side?"

"Don't I get a drink first?" He laughs and strides over to the counter. Five minutes later, he sits down at our table with an expresso, a latte and a donut. We raise our eyes at the selection of foodstuffs.

"I haven't eaten in twenty-four hours. So keep your hands off please."

"What news, Father?" asks Kyla.

The priest shakes his head. "Not good. We can't find it. There is still a presence in the city, but we can't locate it at present. It's like feeling the moisture in the air but there's no rain. But it will rain again soon."

Kyla fills the priest in with developments from our side and I sit brooding on my idea to go to the Saunderson. There's a ton of risk, and no real belief of success, just a shot in the dark.

"Tell him," prompts Kyla. I was lost to the conversation, but I know what she wants. So I relay my idea about the Saunderson building and getting in.

"But we want you to come with us, Father. There's no telling what we could run into or discover. We need someone who understands this stuff. I know how to arrest someone but not how to disarm a demon, monster or whatever this thing is."

"No, you don't," says the priest. "How do you intend on getting in?"

"Well…that's going to take a bit of working out. Like a power cut to the whole building to cut all the CCTV. A proper blowout taking out the back-up generators and the batteries. I don't really know, it's not my field. I usually kick the door down."

"That might not be the best option. There are people in my flock who are expert in these things. Well… they were expert. There's been a change of heart since then. But for a good cause, they might be persuaded. I will need a day, so we should meet tomorrow night."

"Just a day?" asks Kyla.

"We dare not tarry any longer, my child. The rain doesn't stay away forever."

There's a television on the far wall of the coffee house, and right now it is attracting every bit of my attention. It's the twenty-four news channel that's showing, and I can see the Governor standing behind a podium. His lips are moving but there's no sound. Across the bottom of the screen, the missing words are being displayed, and as my eyes scan along the constantly changing text I can feel a chill running down my back.

Less than a day after his wife's death, he is announcing to the world how he has been persuaded to step into the shoes of the current Mayor who has stood down. He's saying how he will bring law and order back to the city. He's letting go a war cry against all injustices, all criminality, and all brutality. There's a threat of curfews and registration of former criminals.

But what is bothering me is none of this. They say that the eyes are the windows of the soul. Through them, you can truly see a person. And it's true, because they don't say it. He says it, his book says it. And I looked into the Governor's eyes today, and they were, if not innocent, then far from evil. But these eyes on the television are different.

"Father," I say, "the Governor?"

"Yes, my son. There's something dwelling within."

23

Chapter 23

Sometimes you need to sleep. My head's pounding as we get to the apartment, and I know with tonight's excursions, I need to get some rest. They say the mind doesn't process everything at once but instead choses quieter moments to think things through. It's as I step through the door that my mind delivers a right hook to the jaw as images of the Chief fill my head.

He was always a pain in the ass, but he was the sort who actually knew his job. If he was on your tail, it wasn't because he was chasing up some chit that hadn't been filled in correctly. It was because you were missing something—and did I ever miss something.

I wonder how they tapped him up, what misdemeanour he had committed which could be exploited. Maybe he had a bit on the side they knew about, or maybe he gambled on the quiet. Or maybe there's worse. Maybe he actually believed in this darkness, was a willing accomplice.

My head's spinning, and my stomach feels a little sick. Kyla's saying something to me, but I'm not listening as I can see him in that chair. The scene was gross, but I'm used to that. No, it's the very idea that he was willing that horrifies me. I drop my jacket and throw myself on the bed. My shoes are removed for me and my socks. It's a little ticklish, but the thoughts in my head are too sad to allow a smirk.

As I lie on my back, eyes closed, I can feel my shirt being undone, but there's no attempt to remove it. There's then a period of rustling and the sound of trousers being dropped. Then the warmth of her skin touches mine, her legs wrapped around mine, thighs and shins touching. Her hair flops against my chest as she brings her own to lie against me. I want to turn and explore this recent angel in my life, but I'm dog tired. So I lie there and drift away.

***

There's a circle of monks, all hooded, before me. They are chanting in a language I don't understand. At the centre of their circle is a child. I'm not sure if it's a boy or girl as from the rear the child seems androgynous. All hoods are focused on the child, and I don't seem to be noticed by them. Some of the monks have chalices in their hands and some have plates with what seems like bread on them.

I look down at my hands and I see a candle which is unlit. In the far corner of the room, we are in is a wooden cross surrounded by metal crosses. But the metal ones are all upside down. A monk moves, and I turn to see him leave the circle. He holds a chalice, but in his other hand is a candle. It's burning. As he walks past me, he turns and inside the cowl I see a face I recognise. It's the Chief, but half his head is missing. I turn in disgust, but curiosity forces me back to see where he is going.

He strides over to beneath one of the metal crosses and lifts the candle up to it. Instantly the light goes out. But there is no fading of the light around the monk. I hear a cry from the child in the circle and quickly focus on the little one. Part of the child's shoulder is in shadow. The rest is lit up normally, but perversely, the light seems unable to penetrate to the child's shoulder.

Another monk leaves the circle, and the same thing happens. This time the child's head is now in shadow as well. And another monk leaves. And another. One after another they go. Soon, all I can see of the child is a foot. But I can hear it wailing.

There's a tap on my shoulder, and I spin round to see Kyla in front of me. She's all in white, holding a candle of her own. There's a smile on her face which lifts me. She takes my free hand with her own. Gently, she leads me towards the wooden cross, and we sit under it opposite each other. I watch her take her candle and hold it up to the cross. It ignites but not with the simple flame like my candle. Instead, there appears to be a miniature raging inferno atop the candle.

The fire is intoxicating, and I struggle to remove my eyes from it. It's only when Kyla places her other hand in mine and then points at my own candle that I realise my stunned immobility. Hesitantly, I raise my own candle and suddenly feel the warmth of the fire that ignites atop it. I look at the flames as they race around each other and lick crazily into the air. There's no steady glow but a wildfire of moods and shades, and a constant warming heat.

The priest is now beside me with his own candle, and he beckons me to follow him. He walks towards the child of whom we can only see the toes of one foot. Carefully, the priest kneels beside the child, and the little one is cast in a flood of light. I run to be beside the priest, and as I hold my candle to the child so the light grows even stronger. I turn for Kyla to join us and am horrified by what I see.

She is on the ground, lying on her belly with one hand holding her candle aloft. With her other arm, she is dragging herself along the floor. Her legs lie immobile behind her and she gasps and grunts as she drags herself towards us. I go to reach for her, but the priest stops me with his free hand and gestures for me to hold my candle close to the child. Slowly, but with every determination, Kyla joins us at the child. And then the light increases again and the warmth of the candles becomes incredibly hot, but strangely bearable.

The monks increase their chanting and then tip their chalices, allowing the red liquid inside to fall to the ground. Then the plates are tipped and what appears to be chunks of flesh land amongst the red liquid that I could swear is blood. There then begins a frenzy as the monks dance on the elements on the floor and begin to spit and swear at them. And then there is a roar.

A raging wind begins around us, and I can feel my face being peppered with what seems to be spittle. However, it has an acidic smell to it, odorous and pungent. And then there is heavy, hungry breathing, like a dog salivating.

"You betray Him, sitting there in your filth. You don't care for Him, you care for yourself. You just want to show them, who you are, show her who you are. You're just a bastard son who wants to see her need you. You want her, you can't stop wanting her. And you should take her. Right now. Use her loneliness, her fear of what's ahead. Control her with it. Take her now, and she'll be yours forever. Be the horny son of a bitch you are. Dominate her! Use her!"

***

I start and sit up in my bed. There's faint light coming in from the window, but my eyes take a moment to adjust, and I can feel myself sweating. The sheets are soaked behind me, and I turn to look at Kyla beside me. I've disturbed the sheets, and I can see every part of her with no clothes to distract.

Inside me, I can feel the animal surging, the one who looks to abandon myself with her. There's a part of me looking to feed my urges on her and racing in my mind are a dozen actions I want to take. She stirs slightly and rolls onto her back exposing her body fully. Dear God, she's so gorgeous, so ripe. Help me.

Kyla continues to roll over and with a thump falls off the bed. I crash back onto my pillows and close my eyes until I hear her get up. She's in front of me in all her glory, and I marvel at her.

"Hey," she says. "I could do with being held."

Dear God, no. I won't resist. I won't be able to stop. I won't…croissants.

"Why don't you go get some croissants? Shop round the corner."

"Okay," she says. As she dresses, I sense she's a little hurt. Better that than what was raging in me. After brushing her hair out and then tying it up, she turns to me.

"Sorry, it's all a bit too fast. I just need someone. Guess I'm kinda scared."

"Hey, don't sweat it. But with all this going on, I just want to make sure that we ain't just looking to exercise out our frustrations. You're too precious for that."

Her eyes stare at me, reading me. After a moment, she begins to smile and that then develops in a wide grin.

"Cool, Mulgrew. That's well cool."

24

Chapter 24

I've never been in a priest's digs, and they're not as I imagined. He's got maps all over the wall and different places marked with crosses and circles. Here and there are pictures of men and sometimes women, some priests or nuns, many not. There are words too. Summonings, rising, mutilation, burnings and various other provocative terms.

Kyla dropped by the retail outlet on the edge of town and picked up some clothes. It's been such a haul since she arrived that it's great to see her wearing something she chose herself instead of hand offs from me. The black leggings with the long shirt and belt look great, especially with the knee length boots. They have a minimal heel, though, so I guess that means they are work boots. Her hair's tied up again, and she looks like a million dollars. Dammit, I feel old using sayings like that.

The priest is not alone when we call. There's a number of rather dubious looking characters, mostly young, mainly male, except for a red headed girl with glasses who's pouring over a computer. There's another character who seems fairly androgynous and the "crew", mostly ex-cons except for the computer girl who is apparently a genius with all this tech stuff. I never knew there was such an underworld amongst the Eastern Europeans, but he says they are all reformed, prepared to fight for a greater cause.

Despite this, the boys seem to take a great delight in Kyla's arrival, and I have to confess, they are looking too intently for my liking. But she soon blows their ideas with her consummate professionalism and cold shoulder.

"The security in the Sanderson is remarkably good, but Janine believes she can fool their camera feed and mask your movements." I give the priest a sharp look as this is our main defence once we get past the door. He nods in response. "She's remarkable. She would have been at Harvard except that her father was a rather loathed man."

"Just keep it safe and simple, Janine. It's our asses up there."

"No worries, Gramps," says Janine.

Am I really getting that old? Nothing like a child to knock the wind out of your sails. There's a sudden smack on my backside, and Kyla snakes round me and plants a strong kiss on my lips, forcing them apart. It's a brief kiss but full of passion.

"Girls, you need to learn to pick'em!" Now I'm feeling like a billion dollars. Her timing's immaculate.

"If we can all just stop the love in for a moment," says the priest. "The boys will create a diversion at the door and get you into the lobby. Head into an elevator, and Janine will be able to cover you from there. Obviously, the longer you remain, the greater likelihood of detection of both you and Janine's activities, but God willing, it'll be enough to see what's going on up there."

"We'll be armed Janine," I say. "But we'll not draw until

necessary, so make sure the cover's good. Guy's, whatever the decoy is, don't stretch it too long, okay? It needs to look genuine. No, it needs to *be* genuine, otherwise they will clear the building, and I don't fancy our chances. Father, are you going in armed?"

The priest raises his eyebrows. "I'll be more heavily armed than you," he says and taps a backpack at his feet. "I wouldn't trust in just a gun."

Kyla spends some time with Janine, going through how she will be covering her tracks while intercepting their camera feed. I take a seat and watch Kyla with Janine, watch her frequent glances and smiles up at me. I had thought my time was done and that maybe I might get lucky with someone of a similar age who wanted to have a companion. Maybe keep the bed warm at night. But Kyla has gotten under my skin. I'm not often blindsided, and when I am, it's usually done so well. I'm not even sure she was aware she was doing it. She's resourceful, caring and stunning. I know that's coming from a dinosaur, but hey, I think I'm right.

The priest taps my shoulder and ushers me into a back room. After closing the door, he points me to a seat and takes one himself. There's a pot of coffee sitting there, and he pours two hot mugs of the steaming black liquid. I take a taste. Java! Well, it'll have to do.

"I haven't really told the others what we will be facing," says the priest, laying back in his seat. "They won't be too close to it and I don't want to scare them."

"What about Kyla?"

"She knows. She's always known since we first met. You realise she has seen this before, to a significant degree. It's got into her mind. I'm amazed she's coming." I stare hard at the priest as Kyla's not been particularly broken, well, in my opinion. In fact, she's been amorous.

"You are a schmuck. She's been really close, hasn't she? I mean, sexually close. She's afraid, and she sees you as a protector. She can't spend the night alone. The quiet is too much. She's in this to get closure. Maybe she will, maybe not. Maybe there will be something bigger."

"Are you saying she's just using me as a sort of comfort blanket?"

"No. But be careful with her. She's a fighter, but inside she's very scared. Don't take her support away."

I take a gulp of coffee and try to focus on the smile she sent me just before I entered this back room.

"What's in the back pack?" That should deflect attention.

"Okay, if you don't want me to talk about her, that's fine. The back pack contains numerous items that should help us against the dark forces. But I don't trust in these things. I trust in the power behind them. That is what you must do too. A gun is nothing without the person behind the trigger. It simply lies there. And so are we. Nothing unless we are used, cared for and pointed."

He sits back, and I see his lips moving.

"What are you doing?"

"Preparing. You should too."

So I do as instructed. Sitting there in silence, I talk into the void with my mind. As much as I try to concentrate on the mission and ask the Big Man for help with that, Kyla keeps coming into the equation. Don't let me cock this up. Don't let me.

25

Chapter 25

It's well-lit around the Saunderson and there's a few couples and groups of people still walking the downtown streets home. They say in a lot of cities that they never sleep, but this one does. Maybe only for a few hours, but it does get its head down. But that time is still a few hours away as I stroll along with Kyla up to the front doors of the Saunderson.

As we approach the front steps, a group of young men barge past us, shouting in a foreign language. I don't recognise it, and it's certainly not Polish. One of them makes straight for the doorman and grabs him in a begging gesture. He pulls his friend from behind him, stumbling, who then falls onto the doorman spilling a copious amount of blood.

Kyla shrieks in my ear, turning her head away from the blood, and I make as if to shield her. There's a couple beside us dressed in rather fine clothes, probably been out to the opera, and I suggest to them that we should step inside away from this rather unsavoury incident.

The commotion with the doorman has brought several

security guards outside, and the rather fine gent suggests to one of them that we could shelter inside. He seems a known figure, and Kyla and I follow in his coat tails inside the lobby. I pull my hat down slightly as I see a camera. Kyla makes for the ladies' rest room, and I saunter past one of the lifts, casually brushing the request button.

The door opens as I loiter and I see a lift operator inside. A couple enter the lift and I make excuses about waiting for my wife. As soon as its doors close, I press again for another lift. From the corner of my eye, I see the commotion outside has grown and there's the flashing lights of an ambulance. A frail old man is helped inside by a security guard and hobbles his way over to one of the lifts.

"Is the next one taken, son?"

"No, it's okay sir," I reply. "It's all yours."

"Please accompany me," croaks the voice. It's then I realise, as the voice loses that croaking edge, that I am looking at the priest. It's a stunning disguise. The lift doors open, and Kyla is also exiting the ladies rest room. I help the priest into the lift which is attended by a young woman dressed in a smart golden uniform. As we enter, the priest stumbles into her and stabs out a finger on the control panel to close the doors. As they shut behind us Kyla has placed a cloth over the girl's face which has enough sedative on it to keep her under for a few hours. Through the ever decreasing gap, I see that the outside commotion has begun to quieten. So far so good.

Kyla lays the girl down on the floor, and the priest strips away his garb to reveal an all black ensemble underneath. He puts a balaclava over his face and indicates for us to don our own.

Without any prompt from inside the elevator, it begins to

move upwards, and I pray that this is Janine causing this and that we haven't been rumbled already. There's no time to think that way, and I pull my handgun from its discrete holster. Kyla takes hold of hers too. We cast a glance at each other, but all I see are resolute eyes.

The doors open, and we point our guns out into the hallway which is barely lit. Moving and covering each other, we secure the hallway for the priest to exit, but he ignores what we are doing and stops like an open target in the hallway. After a moment, he points upward to the ceiling. Then he strides off along the corridor.

We high tail it after him until we reach a corner. Here he stops and holds up his hands. There's a brief muttering from the priest, and we hear two groans and two dull thuds like a sack of potatoes crashing to the ground. The priest starts walking again, and we pass two unconscious guards in smart suits. They seem enormous despite their prone position, and I'm glad the priest did whatever he did.

There's a staircase ahead, and we climb it at pace before the priest abruptly stops again. Once more there's mutterings, and the sound of fallen bodies. I'm more than a little surprised by this turn of events, but there's no time to think about that now. We move on until another corridor comes into view.

There's movement around this corner, and the priest kneels on the floor. He takes his backpack and removes two knives from it, handing them to Kyla and myself. He takes a short sword for himself.

"Don't let your eyes stop you. Around this corner are spirits, thoroughly evil. Whatever they present themselves as, don't hesitate to use the knives on them. I nod, as does Kyla, and we brace ourselves. With a quick hand motion from the priest, we quickly turn the corner.

There are two young girls in the corridor, both wearing pink and white frocks with large lollipops in their hands. As I reach forward with my dagger, I find myself pulling back, steering my anger away from the children before me. One touches me, and I feel a sharp pain. I begin to reel and Kyla moves across to catch me. I barely see the priest as he rushes past us, despatching what seems to me to be two lovely girls in Sunday dress. And then an agonised face rushes before us before disappearing into the darkness.

"I told you to do it. Don't back down whatever you see."

The priest marches on, and as we round another corridor's end, I can hear people chanting. Actually, it's more like a drone, there's no tune or real substance. It's like the whole joy has been removed.

The corridor ends in a pair of double doors with an open cupboard door beside it. Beyond the double doors comes the droning and the cries of a woman under torture. A glance at the cupboard beside reveals a large number of knives and corkscrews.

"They're torturing someone," I whisper.

But the priest shakes his head. "Not torturing. Marking. Carving all the vulgarities of the day. They are cursing her in a way you can't even begin to know!"

26

Chapter 26

"Are we going to get in there and save her?" asks Kyla, but the priest holds up a hand.

"We'll need to see how many and what else is in there."

"What else?" I murmur.

"If there's only people, we'll be lucky."

I see Kyla close her eyes and begin to draw her face in what seems to be a sign of pain. The priest is watching her closely, and he begins to nod.

"Just as I thought," he says, "There are some other spirits in there. We need to be careful and not just run in."

Another scream from the victim reaches our hiding place, and I can see Kyla flinch. She's not comfortable just waiting.

"We need to get her."

"Wait here. We need to understand," says the priest.

"Kyla, I think we should hold…."

But it's too late. She stands up and kicks in the door in front of us, running inside as it swings open. I see the priest's look of horror as I stand and follow my partner into the room.

The room has little light in it except for one small spotlight in the centre of the room located in the ceiling. Beneath this spotlight, hanging upside down is the governor's wife. There's a sharp kick of incomprehension in my mind before the rest of the scene is taken in. There must be at least twenty of them in monk's habit, black in colour as before. A few are drawing weapons. I see a handgun, a sword, and knives. There's a sound, and I see the spark of a gun firing on my right side. There's another retort of a handgun, the sound that Kyla's gun would make. A body falls to the ground.

I open fire at the monks converging on me, hitting at least two. My aim's usually poor, and I reckon neither shot is good enough to kill. I spin round as I am approached from behind and deliver a punch followed by a knee to the groin to my assailant. The priest rushes past me, shouting out in a language I don't understand with a long stick that seems to be on fire.

Kyla grunts as she is hit by a rather large monk, and I tag him in the shoulder with my gun. He spins away and begins to run. I then feel the scratch of sharp nails across my face and turn to see those eyes of rage I saw at the wildlife park. A hand turns me and something else appears before me. It is faint, but has a face of sorts, certainly a mouth for it screams out obscenities in my face. Then an arm, long and more like an insect's appendage rather than a human arm, drives into my forehead. And everything goes black.

***

It's late autumn and there's leaves on the ground. A myriad of browns and reds they seem to almost be on fire as they swirl in the wind. I can see the lake. It's back home, where I grew up, back in Ireland. I see the house where I was brought up. Well it's not the house that I remember. Instead it's a ruin that has the dimensions of it. But all the outside paint had peeled. Slates have fallen from the roof leaving it half exposed. The windows are smashed with glass lying around.

There's a scream coming from inside the building. I run, in bare feet, to the front door which is half hanging off its hinges. The glass from the door's broken panes cuts my feet, but I continue. Inside there's family photos tossed to the floor, paper peeling from the walls. In a corner, all my accolades and awards lie broken on the carpet which is sodden. I don't remember ever winning that many, but part of me knows they are mine.

The scream comes again and I rush into the next room to see a man standing there. He's at least seven foot tall and built like a wrestler on supplements. His skin is red in colour, like nothing I have ever seen. But his eyes are blank. I mean they are there, but there's no iris just a white ball in the socket. And at his feet is a woman knelt on the ground. The shape and size makes me wonder. And then I know, I just know.

He grabs the woman by her black hair turning her to me. It's Kyla, and she's bare but there is nothing erotic about her appearance. She's looks terrified and broken. Her face is a mess of running mascara and bruises. Her body too has cuts and open wounds all over it.

"She was adequate, but the next one will be better," says a voice and then laughs knowingly. The man's mouth hasn't opened, but I know it's him. He stamps his foot and part of the floor falls away. I can see into it, and there are several women there. Jenny, Hughes, Sarah my first love from school, still at that age and also my mother.

There is nothing but anger and rage in me, and I race at the man, but he catches me in one hand by the neck and lifts me off my feet.

"And you can watch." There is laughter, raucous laughter.

***

Kyla is slapping my face. Real hard too.

"Wake up! Bloody wake up. I can't carry you."

I lurch forward, shaking my head to clear it. There's still darkness around. I hear the priest calling things out. We're still in that room. I glance and see the woman still hanging upside down.

"Some have left the room, my child," says the priest to Kyla. "We need to get out of here.

"If they come up from below, we're going to be in a firefight that we won't win," shouts Kyla above the noise of rushing monks. They seem to be coming close but are then repelled. I don't understand one iota what's happening.

"What are they doing?" asks Kyla. Beyond us are spirits swirling around. They are like ghosts and fire combined. And beyond them, the monks are packing up everything they can get their hands on. The cupboard outside sounds like it is being emptied.

"The doors..," I stutter, "they must be open if they are clearing out the cupboard."

"We can't move, Mulgrew," says Kyla, "it's only the priest's force field that's keeping us safe so far."

"Force field?"

"They are leaving!" yells the priest. Beyond us I can see holes opening up in the air and other places seem to lie beyond them. There are rooms, streets, beaches and parks. But one monk is standing still and performing some sort of ritual. From the floor in front of the monk rises up a tongue of fire which then begins to form into a bird. It starts to fly round the room letting out bursts of fire, setting everything alight. The bird then comes towards us and pours fire onto us which is deflected by the force field.

"They mean to trap us in this inferno," says Kyla. "We need to get out."

I can hear the tortured woman screaming as flames from the room strike her. As he looks around the room, I sense the priest is starting to panic. Groggily I get to my feet.

"Have you anything to strike that bird with?"

"No, it's all I can do to keep us shielded."

"Then drop it and get ready to run. I'll distract it. Get out and get Kyla out! Don't wait for me."

The priest doesn't hesitate, and I run straight at the bird before diving to one side. I feel a blast of fire across my back and guess that my coat is burning. I pull it off me throwing it away and roll to one side as another blast comes my way.

"Mulgrew!"

I turn to see Kyla and the priest disappear through one of the openings. There are very few monks left now and only a few openings remaining. I'm thinking about diving through the nearest one but a scream jolts me to the realisation that the governor's wife is still alive.

Twisting as a blast of fire comes at me, I feel my hat catch fire and fling it away. There is only one opening left now and one monk who is turning to leave through that opening. I can see a beach through it and can even hear the sound of the sea.

The bird hovers in front of me waiting for my move. The opening is closing as the monk moves towards it. Feinting to one side I then push off in the opposite direction. Fortunately, the opening is close to the stricken governor's wife and I charge straight at her. I jump and swing with her on the rope into the opening which the monk is climbing through. All three of us clatter together through the opening which shuts cutting the rope holding the governor's wife.

As I taste sand in my mouth, I feel a scrab of nails across the back of my neck.

27

Chapter 27

It's a soft sand and my fall's also broken by the governor's wife beneath me. She's in a mess, groaning but struggling to move except that she is shaking from the incredible pain she must be in. And I'm feeling pain too as sharp nails repeatedly drag across my neck. The pain is acute enough to make me think that blood's being drawn.

My assailant is on my back and I'm jammed between two bodies. I try to struggle clear but it isn't working, so I grab a handful of sand and fling it behind me, approximating where the neck gorger's head is. It works to a degree as I feel the body above lessen its weight and rock. This allows me to roll and throw the mad monk off.

As I get clear, I scramble to my feet, forcing myself upward, my feet slipping through the sand. Opposite me, the monk rises too but the cowl has dropped behind and I see the face of my attacker. The wild eyes are surrounded by red hair, curled and tangled. Her skin is white and the habit is open revealing a taut body. But the eyes take every thought of beauty from her.

I watch her right hand move, and she produces a knife from within her habit. Stepping forward, she reveals a milky white thigh. It looks strong and toned, and I begin to fear she may be a fighter of some sort. Glancing down at the governor's wife, I see someone dying and I know I haven't got a lot of time. If only Kyla was here.

The monk moves, very quickly and swipes across my chest with the blade, which I manage to evade, but she kicks me hard in the chest, sending me pummelling backwards. Rolling to one side, I avoid her follow up and scramble away desperately thinking how to beat this evil woman.

"I'll gut you. Hang your entrails out to dry in the sun before skinning you alive. He'll enjoy you, will want a piece of you."

"Who will?" I cry, more to give me a few moments to grab a breath than from any curiosity. She responds, but I don't know the language, and my confusion must be evident as she follows with, "The Darkness. Night is falling and the stars won't shine." This time it's a kick to my head, and I throw my hands up, which fortunately take the full brunt of the kick.

I look around for a weapon, any weapon, there's got to be one here somewhere. This time it's a punch to the ribs, and I feel the wind getting knocked from me with the follow-up. She's getting cocky now and taunting me, which is good. No, really, it is, as she's got the beating of me any day. This time she's lazy and walks in towards me, and I feign injury, hunched on one knee.

"You're a pitiful excuse. You're not worth gutting. I think I'll just rip out your…"

I drive a punch into her midriff as I rise up and then grab her red hair and pull it hard, dragging her head down to the sand. I follow with a couple of punches to the head but only one really catches. Then there's a cry.

"Freeze. Police! Everyone get your hands up."

I back off slowly, not taking my eyes off the monk. She rises too, and her eyes are full of pain.

"Officer, thank god you are here. He was trying to rape me. Another minute, and I would have been trapped beneath him…"

"I doubt Detective Trimble would do such a thing."

I recognise the voice but can't put a face to it. My curiosity gets the better of me, and I turn to see a young man. He's in casual clothes, and I don't recognise him as one of ours. But then my mind sees him in a uniform and the image clicks.

"Huntingdon? Glad you were passing." He's holding a handgun which is pointed at the monk, but she's still giving it the sob story. He doesn't flinch, but instead instructs her to lie on the ground. She opens the habit and then lies face down before pulling the cowl over her head. Then her arms and hands move inside the habit.

"What the..?" Huntingdon is open mouthed in disbelief. I watch as the habit begins to flatten out like a tyre deflating. I race forward and grab the garment only to find it empty.

"Damn! Huntingdon, get an ambulance and the rest of the gang down here. She's bound to have left some sort of forensics. Huntingdon! Are you listening?"

But he's just staring at the sand and the habit. I shout at him again, and he then pulls out a phone and begins to discharge my instructions. I turn to the governor's wife. She's barely breathing. I look around me, and it's still dark. I soon get my bearings and realise we are just outside the city. I pull my phone from my pocket. Within a minute, I have Kyla speaking at the other end. She's tells me several times she's glad I'm alive. And I reciprocate before the helicopter for the medical evacuation of the governor's wife drowns out all communication.

Chapter 28

"I'm staying here! I don't care if you think I need a check up, I'm staying right here until she wakes up."

The doctor looks at me as if I am insane. His thoughts are probably governed by the two plain clothes officers at the door posted by the temporary Chief. At least he bought my idea that we shouldn't informing people until we had a positive identification.

"I will need to examine you, though. For your own good."

"Fine doctor, but not until some of my colleagues get here."

"Won't the ones at the door do?" he asks. It's a reasonable statement and hard to give an unsuspicious answer too so I don't try to explain.

"No. Sorry, Doc, but no."

"Okay, Detective, let the nurse at the ward desk know when you are available."

I nod and turn to drink some of the plastic cup coffee from the vending machine. It's utter shit, but it's warm, and warm is good at the moment. Kyla's on her way as well as the temporary Chief. It's a difficult time at the moment knowing who to trust. The new Chief was kosher with regard to keeping the discovery of a once-dead-women-now-alive under wraps. If they know she's still alive, they will come for her. But who's to know if they can't track her anyway?

The temporary Chief also sent a squad down to the now burnt out Saunderson building. Well, burnt out is an exaggeration. There was serious fire damage to several floors, but the floors seemed strangely empty. There were no signs of any cults or secret societies. Hughes and Gonzales were on the team down there, so if the force is involved in the cover up then it's a damn good cover up.

I look out of the window. St. Andrew's Hospital is a tall sky scraper of a building with a helipad on top located close to the centre of the city. It has the best facilities and eight hours ago its best doctors performed surgery on the woman in the bed beside me. No one mentioned anything unusual except for the marks around her neck like she had been hung at some point.

I'd like to get to the morgue and see if there's a body there, but at the moment I don't want to arouse any suspicions in case they come for her. After all our chasing and running about this women, dead or alive, zombie or whatever she is now that she's breathing again, is our best hope of getting some answers as to what the real plan is.

There's a stirring in the bed behind me, and I turn and see the woman lying there open her eyes. Her first name is Diana something I gleaned from the charts at the end of the bed. For a detective, I can be pretty rubbish with detail, especially names. Faces I don't forget, but names are another issue.

I take a plastic cup of water from a side unit as Diana starts to cough, and I gently allow her to sip it. After a moment, she begins to scan the room desperately, looking for something.

"They're not here. You're safe, Diana. You're many floors up in St Andrews and I have the room protected."

"Safe?" She gives out a weak laugh. "You think I'm safe. I was dead, and they came after me."

"Who did? And what do they want?"

She laughs again, a wild cackle like I have missed the joke. "They want it all. The city. We were going to rule over it. My husband and I. But now they want him because I screwed up. They don't tolerate failure. They don't tolerate anything except obedience."

"Who doesn't?"

"They. The Darkness, all of them."

"Who is the Darkness?" I ask. She laughs again.

"There are a few of us on their council."

"Politicians?" Again she laughs.

"Humans. The rest are from the other world."

I let this comment slide despite the connotations it puts into my head. "Who are they? The humans."

"I don't know. When we meet we all wear the habits with the cowls. If your cowl is removed you are in trouble. Not even death can keep you safe." She laughs again, her mind seemingly reeling.

"Where do they meet?"

"You can't stop them. There's no point to trying. You should run, get clear from here. It'll be worse for you." She coughs again, spitting up a little blood. "They'll take it all over. Sodom right here in the city. A glorious testimony to His Unholiness."

Her body is starting to shake now. But this isn't some sort of fit, rather it's like a fight to retain control of it. She's looking ahead and can see something.

"No!" she yells at the air. The footsteps of the guards at the door can be heard briefly before the door slams shut. They begin banging on the door but I am focused on Diana who has begun to levitate, lifting her covers into the air. I try to push her down, but it's a constant struggle.

"No! Not you!" She's spitting into the air in front of her. "I worked for you, I made him follow you." Her mouth is full of blood which she coughs up in between words of hate at her invisible aggressor. "You bastard, you cowardly bastard, sending him."

She turns her head to me trying to speak but the blood she's coughing up now is choking her. I lean in close to her mouth and hear something. "Fear gerty-coo." She gurgles and I feel the blood spattering into the side of my face. Her arm swings at me and knocks me with extra-ordinary force across the room. Shaking my head, I try to stand but find myself groggy. I check the door and see two faces peering in. The guards are still pulling at the door but are astonished at what they see.

Diana rotates in the air, her feet stopping just before the floor. The covers fall off and she floats over to me. I manage to stand and am instantly grabbed by her hands pulling me right up to her face.

"See you in Hell, Trimble." It's not her voice but a deep one which rumbles. I'm dropped to the floor, and she turns in the air. With barely a moment's pause, she rotates until she is horizontal. Then like the firing of a cannon, she races head first through the window, shattering it.

I run to the broken window, crunching glass underfoot and hear the door behind me burst open.

"What the hell did you do to her?"

"Don't be such an idiot," I chastise the guard. Looking down

I see her broken body which has fallen a full twenty-five stories. Her limbs lie in a configuration that certainly isn't healthy, and there's blood splattered everywhere. I begin to think that is that until I see her head begin to move and twist until it is looking back up at me. She laughs, deep and callous, somehow ringing in my ears though I am so high above, before trying to lift herself up from the ground.

"Get out of my way!" I knock the guards to one side and sprint out of the room, desperately seeking the stairs. There's a sign ahead, and I follow the blue arrows, bursting the door open to the descending steps. I take them two at a time, sometimes three. I reckon I get out of the building in less than two minutes. Flinging open the last door to the open air I see a gruesome sight.

"Time for her to burn!"

Diana's body is laughing at me and even taunting me. It is making its way in stuttered steps and sudden lurches towards the incinerator building. Well, not on my watch. I race towards Diana but something catches me a serious crack to the face. My nose begins to pour blood as I fall to the floor.

Meanwhile, Diana continues her sorry passage to the incinerator. Between us, I see a slight ripple in the view like looking through steam. Drawing my weapon, I fire at Diana, and she topples forward slightly before regaining her balance. I get to my feet and run after her, but then see a change in the view. It's a sudden blurring, and I instantly duck. I can hear the punch swing over me. Diana is through the door now, and I follow as fast as I can, but something gets past me.

As I run down a corridor following the blood stained footprints of Diana, I see hospital workers thrown to the side, here and there. Rounding a corner, I enter the furnace room and see solid metal door to the burner being opened by no one. I fire off a few rounds at where I suspect the invisible creature to be, but there is no connection. Hell, who knows if you can even shoot it?

A black, charred, metal tray is pulled out, and Diana starts to climb on board. She lies down flat, but then sits up backwards, that is her spine cracks as she forms an "L" shape but the wrong way round to normal. Her head then turns round to face me at an impossible angle, more akin to an owl. And she howls with laughter!

"Be seeing you, Detective, I want to watch you burn too." And she laughs and laughs. I turn as the flames start to burn the body. That's the door closing shut.

29

Chapter 29

I end up downtown giving statements for about two hours. The temporary Chief is in the room and giving me a look as if I am mad until someone comes in with a file. I'm guessing it must be the reports of the two guards. Still, he looks pretty pissed. After a while, he tells the two detectives in the room with him to leave.

"The camera's off, Trimble, because you and I need to have a talk." He's a thin man, rather tall and has slightly greying hair. He sweeps it back with his left hand, and I can see the sweat stains on his shirt under his armpit. There's a slight tremor in his hand, but he's holding it together well, all things considering.

"These things you have seen, Trimble, how do you suggest we take them further? I mean with they are, how do we... deal with them?"

"We need to find where they are meeting. I am inclined to tail everyone who resides in the Saunderson to see if we can ace any of these meetings. I don't know what we'll encounter when we do, but there could be a lot of trouble so I'd hit it with force." I keep my face grim and determined.

"Trimble, do you have any idea how I would justify that? Tail some of this city's most important and influential people because a dead woman told you about some society that's out to do the city ill in conjunction with things from elsewhere." He's shaking as he speaks.

"I know what I saw, and I think the two guards corroborated my story. You can bring in the orthodox priest and Corstain, they'll back me up." I'm well aware of the fantastical story I'm telling, but the stakes are too high now."

"I have an open air shooting, child sacrifice, dead women walking and a police chief being controlled by them. I'll either be committed, laughed at, or possibly worse, be giving a heads up to the forces behind all this that we are serious and coming for them." He reaches for a cup of water and spills some as he takes it to his lips.

"Look sir, I know it's hard to…"

"Mulgrew! I believe you. That's what's making me nervous. You are casting doubt on my being able to go to any higher authority. Who's to say that the people above me ain't involved?" He stares away to the wall. "At this time, I'd prefer to keep everything close to our chest. Keep people away from our investigations."

"I understand, sir, but what have we got to go on? The Saunderson was where it took place. So there we start. Tailing them. Some of them there must be involved."

"Was there anything else said by Diana? Any clue?"

I pause to think. At times like these, it's always good to reflect. And my first reflection is I just said "times like these". When have I seen a time like this? I try to replay Diana's last moments. There was something…up in the hospital room.

She tried to tell me something. It came out garbled.

"Yes, sir, there was something. Before she took her flying trip she said something to me after we were talking about the people involved. She said, *Fear, gearty-coo*."

"Was she compromised?"

"Just a little. There was some invisible spirit or something in front of her. She was shouting at it one minute, babbling this the next."

He's staring at the ceiling now and stroking his chin. I don't know whether or not to trust him. Is he trying to keep me away from the Saunderson crowd because he's in league with them, or is he just being sensible and keeping us below cover? He's making funny shapes with his mouth, trying out different connotations of speaking by the look of it. There's a few shakes of the head.

"The docks, Trimble, that's where we need to be, the docks."

"Sir?"

"Pier Thirty-two. I was trying to see how sounds would be if my mouth was impeded in some way and Pier Thirty-two is what came to mind."

"Sir?"

"Fear, gearty-coo. Pier Thirty-two."

"Ah! With you now, sir." The more I chew it over in my mind, the more it seems to make sense, although that may be just me clutching at straws.

"Go home, Trimble. You need some rest before your night ops tonight."

"Yes, sir."

Walking out of the interview room, I spot Hughes and wave her over. I relate the conversation I have just had and ask for her opinion.

"He's a solid guy, and I haven't ever seen anything of him that would make me question his integrity," she says.

I nod. "I understand, Hughes, but I would have said the same about the Chief before he fed me to the wolves.

"So you think this could be a trap?"

"Maybe," I agree, "or maybe the guy's a clever little cookie and is really onto something. Either way, it's a risk I think we need to take. If we can get into a part of the network without them knowing, we could maybe see a way to take them down. Or maybe even see how their end game plays out."

"I'll brief Gonzales. Shall we go from your place?"

"Yes. Full undercover. Make sure the armoury's in the boot."

I take a shower before heading to the shooting range. Nothing pains me more than drawing my weapon but it's advisable to keep it in trim at this time. I spend an hour there, focused and thinking about nothing but the other end of the range. Strangely for me, I find it the most relaxing thing I have done in days. Times must be bad.

A pair of arms slip around me as I take my coat out of my locker.

"Thank God you're safe. I had no idea where you'd gone."

I let the arms tighten and squeeze for a moment before turning round and embracing Kyla fully. She plants a kiss on my cheek before thinking better of it and forcing her way into my mouth. I lied about the shooting range. This is better.

"We need to go to bed," I tell her.

"I'm not that sort of girl," she says. "I prefer to wait until things are permanent." There's a little shock on her face at my statement.

"We have a night op, Kyla. I wasn't asking for anything." She giggles. It's so good to see her laugh. I brief her in the car on the way back to the apartment, and there's a look of worry on her face.

"We should take the priest again. He's got a handle on these things that we don't."

"Okay," I agree, "you ring him and tell to meet us at my place."

She tries three times, but there's no answer from his cell phone. Neither does anyone else know where he is at the cathedral or his office. Kyla says she'll try again when we get up. Something is kicking me at the back of my mind, but I need rest so I continue back to the apartment.

Kyla showers whilst I, the dirty pig that I am, just strip down to my boxers and fall into bed. I'm drifting when I fell the arms encircle me again. Her light breath on my back is soothing as her hands move up and down my chest. She pulls herself closer, and I can fell the full length of her body against me. A leg snakes around mine, and I realise she has found a comfortable position as her breathing begins to ease. Hell, it's not that comfortable for me, but I'm sure I'll drop off at some point. Don't really feel like kicking her out.

30

Chapter 30

We're up an hour before Hughes arrives with Gonzales. Black is the order of the day as I look around my little team, and I feel a dread come over me. We're so few compared to this thing that's going on. But there's nothing else for it. Kyla tried the priest again, but no one has seen him recently.

The docks can sometimes be a busy place, even at night, but Hughes has a roster for vessel movements, and there's nothing around pier thirty-two all night. It would have been good to have had a watch on the pier all day, but as this was the only piece of intel we had, the risk of some daft new beat getting spotted looking about was too great. And if we went outside the team, who knows what leaks there might have been.

It's hard trusting virtually no one.

"How do we play this, Trimble?" asks Hughes. "What are we looking for when we get inside?"

"Anything of use. I really don't know," I say. "We also need to be careful in case this is a trap. We could walk in on a large group or find nothing. It's a real shot in the dark, but it's all we have even after all the troubles."

"If we need to, we'll split up as well," says Kyla. "Photograph only and try not to disturb anything. If we can get a look at these guys without them knowing, then we might finally get a step ahead instead of playing catch up all the time."

Moving out to the car, we try to act casual, but I realise everyone is in black. We look like a particularly energetic funeral party, and that's without the hoods. Fortunately, there isn't many people about the area at one in the morning.

The car ride is uneventful, and we park at the roadside a small walk from the pier. There are lights across the way at the larger piers where vessels are being loaded and unloaded. There's a general warming effect so that we ain't walking in total darkness, and I lead the team away from any lights.

The tide can be heard lapping gently against the large wooden struts of the pier, and as we get to pier thirty-two, I realise just how small it is. Apart from a small loading crane, suitable for a minor fishing vessel to be loaded with, there is only a tiny wooden hut on the pier. The outside has flaking paint and there's a door with glass panels and a large window at the front. We sneak up in the dark to behind the hut, and Gonzales jukes round to see if anyone is inside.

"Clear," he says.

"Open it."

After examining his selection of lock picking tools, Gonzales spends three minutes opening the door. There's no electricity coming into the hut, and I step inside fairly confident that there are no alarms.

There's a small wooden table covered in fishing magazines, some old twine sitting on top of these and some plastic buckets beside a rickety chair. And that's it. The overall feeling is one of disuse.

"Guess it's a dead end," says Hughes, shouldering her shotgun.

"Looks like it," I agree.

"Boss, the door lock and the door itself, the way it moves and the fact that the lock is well oiled doesn't seem to align with that. Some things seem maintained better than the general repair of the place indicates."

I trust what Gonzales says, but it's hard to think that this is anything but a mainly unused pier hut. Regardless, I decide to search the walls, thin and wooden as they are. As I move down one side, it seems strange to check out what are basically planks of wood forming a hut side. I can feel the roughness of them and the bend as I push hard at them, but they seem firm enough to maintain the hut integrity.

"Over here," says Kyla. She's at the farthest corner of the hut, and she's hard to make out clearly. As I approach, I notice that her left hand is leaning on the outside wall but that her right hand has disappeared into the wood up to her wrist.

"Woah, Kyla! That's not normal, be careful."

Hughes withdraws her shotgun and pushes the barrel into the wood and watches it disappear. Retrieving it, she then repeats the procedure many times. Kyla watches, and then seemingly satisfied, pushes her head into the wood and it disappears. I wait for a few moments, then tap her shoulder. Her head re-emerges.

"You gotta see this, Mulgrew!"

I step past her and push my head into the wood. There's a weird tingle round my neck and then my head has emerged through the other side. Looking around, I see what I would expect if I had broken down the wall. There's the pier edge leading down to the water. Ahead of me there are other pier lights in the distance. Above is a cloudy sky with a touch of moonlight tickling the edges. But in front of me is a ladder. It's clear, almost like looking at very pure ice. The rungs start at my chest and then descend down into the water.

I touch the top rung, and it feels solid. Grabbing the next one down as well, I give the ladder a shake but it is unmoveable. I place my left leg on a rung, and let it support my weight. Again, it feels secure.

Returning into the hut, I see expectant faces.

"Well there's a ladder out there."

"I saw no ladder," says Hughes.

"No you didn't, and neither did I. This is a very weird ladder which seems to descend into the sea." I'm aware this is not the most enthralling way to describe what I have seen, but I'm trying not to get anyone overly excited or worried about this turn of events. And the person I'm thinking of is me!

"We don't know where it goes," says Hughes. "It could be dangerous, a trap as you said before."

"But it could be answers," says Kyla."

"And we need answers," I say. "We damn well need answers!"

"What are we going to do?" asks Gonzales.

I look him back in the eye. "We're going to get some answers!"

31

Chapter 31

Given her prowess at fighting, Kyla is taking the lead with Hughes and her shotgun following right behind. I'm like the slightly useless leader in the middle while Gonzales has the rear. I'm not happy about Kyla at the front, but it does make sense.

Stepping through the wall, I take my place on the ladder and follow Hughes down it. There's something bizarre about being in the open and yet not in the open. I expect wind, to feel the cold, but there's nothing, almost like being on one of those simulators for rollercoasters: They can throw you around all they want, but without the outside elements hitting your face, they miss the mark.

The descent takes a couple of minutes and that, I believe, puts us below the pier and quite likely below the seabed at the harbour. As we reach the floor, we are in a small cubed room with only the one exit and coupe of gas canisters to one side. The door's metal, and there's no decoration on the concrete walls.

I nod at Kyla, and she opens the door. Beyond is a dimly lit corridor, but this has style about it. The walls are papered and there's a carpet on the floor, possibly Axminster, but I'm no expert. I can see paintings along the walls, but at the current angle, I can't see what detail there is.

"I can't see any signs of electronic surveillance or security system," whispers Kyla.

I give Hughes a questioning glance, and she nods in confirmation. I think back to the Saunderson and how it had all these modern means of detection except on the floors occupied by these strange monks. And then I think of their forms of protection. Spirits and demons. Who needs electronics?

I wave my hand indicating we move on. Kyla with her weapon drawn moves so lightly on her feet. Hughes beside her now is less delicate but soundless all the same. Kyla gives a start and I see her eye has caught the image in one of the paintings. There's a demon—well I think it's a demon—standing over the body of what I presume was a man. It appears it was suppertime. The image is gross yet compelling. It's like the demon's eyes are already looking at you, into you.

Drawing my attention away, I motion us to move on. There's a door on our left hand side now and Kyla and Hughes take up position. Trying the handle, Kyla finds it moves freely and twists it gently. The door swings open, and I sense the women tense slightly and then relax.

"Toilet," whispers Kyla. I guess even evil monks need a pee.

We move on and there's more paintings on either side. One has a truly blasphemous image of God but most show cruelty to man. In each one, the eyes of the main protagonist, usually a demon or horror creature, seem to glare at you as you look. I feel tremors inside like I was facing the real thing.

The next door is on the left, and again Kyla and Hughes

carry out a standard entry. This door leads to what appears to be a waiting room. There are a number seats around the sides of the room and a door in the far corner. Otherwise the room is fairly plain except for cross on the floor. Entering from the corridor, it displays as upside down.

"Gonzales, cover the corridor. Corstain, Hughes, through that door."

Another textbook entry gives way to what seems to be a private study. There's an impressive oak desk in the middle of the room with two basic chairs sat before it and an impressive red velvet chair, covered with ornate carvings, sitting behind it. The carvings are of demon faces and unholy signs. A large portrait adorns the wall behind the basic chairs and shows the face of something so grotesque, I wonder how anyone managed to look at it for long enough to paint it.

There's drawers in the desk," says Hughes. "And some filing cabinets behind." Without asking, she begins to fiddle with the handle of one of the drawers. I hear a little "pfft" sound, like wind from a puffer, and Hughes falls to the ground. I motion Kyla to cover the door and reach down to her neck. There's a pulse but there's also a small needle.

Using the edge of my garments, I pick out the needle and wrap it into my sleeve. My mind races about what to do. I have no idea what has been placed into Hughes' system, how deadly it is or even if he will make it out of the room alive. Conversely, is it just a stun dart, leaving you for whoever comes?

Without warning, Kyla bends over holding her head. I leave Hughes and grab Kyla by the shoulders.

"What is it?" I whisper.

"Something's here. Just arrived. I think it's coming this way."

"Is it the killer? That demon who took all those people apart."

"No, it's different. The feelings not as strong, but it's there. And it's getting stronger. Warn Gonzales!"

I stick my head out the door and call over Gonzales. On hearing of our plight, he asks what we should do. And that really stumps me. If it were the monks, we could shoot our way out, but we don't even know if our weapons will work on what's coming.

"Hide!"

"Where?" Gonzales replies.

I drag him into the study, closing the door behind us. Kyla is still holding her head, and I tell him to get under the desk. His face is shocked as he sees Hughes on the floor, but I tell him to get her under too. I take Kyla by the shoulders and lead her beside Gonzales, and we all huddle together.

I'm holding Hughes' shotgun, and Gonzales has his handgun ready. Kyla is shaking, holding her head like it's about to explode. Then we hear the thudding. It's coming from the corridor, best I can tell, and sounds like someone, or something hopping along.

Gonzales watches my face as the sound of hopping feet gets closer. I try to keep a grim but resolved look on my face. Inside, I'm so scared. My stomach is tossing, and it feels like I might soil my pants with fear.

The thudding stops momentarily, and then sounds like it is coming from the next room. Bollocks, we left the door to the corridor open. And then the study door swings open. There's a hop. Thud. Another. Thud. From under the desk, I can see the feet of whatever is before us. They look like the talons of an eagle but are red. A wing dips into view with a small claw on it. Judging by the feet, if you reckon on its feet, and human feet being equivalent, the thing must be seven feet tall.

And then a beak shows under the desk. And then an eye.

32

Chapter 32

Poking the nose of the shotgun out under the desk, I let go with both barrels. There's an insane howl from the creature which is lifted across the small room into the far wall. Green blood smatters the room I tell Gonzales to get Hughes and go. He's a wiry but strong figure and has her over his shoulder and begins to run for the corridor.

I reload and push through the gap under the desk to see the aberration that has come looking for us. It has wings, black and scaly, and an incredibly powerful looking beak. My ears are screaming for mercy at the sound it's making, but I dare not take my hands off the gun.

I hear Kyla getting up behind me, half sobbing, half yelling at the creature to go away.

"Follow Gonzales! Get back up the ladder and go." But Kyla doesn't take heed and starts to shoot at the drawers in the desk.

"We can't leave with nothing," she yells above the creature's cries.

It's beginning to come around now, and the creature looks at me before swinging a wing towards me. I empty both barrels again but the wing catches me, throwing me into the wall with incredible force. I drop the shotgun and fall to the ground. My ribs feel like a car has just driven into them, but my legs feel remarkably good considering. Getting to my feet, I go to leave but realise Kyla's still shooting at the drawers.

"Open! Bloody hell, just flaming open!"

She's totally distracted, and the bird makes towards her. I'm unarmed, but that monstrosity is not going to take Kyla. I jump onto its back and grab at the wing. It turns its head like an owl and pecks me hard in the shoulder. I can feel the skin break and then blood starts to seep into my outfit. The clothing's colour hides the distinct stain that lighter clothes would show, but I can feel I'm bleeding.

The creature turns at Kyla who has now recognised the danger. As she points her weapon, the bird strikes her arm with its beak and sends the firearm flying across the room. I see the creature peck at Kyla, but she sidesteps and delivers two quite punishing blows to its head. There's little effect, and it reaches a claw and grabs Kyla by the leg.

Kyla's firearm has slid past me, and I reach for it. Turning back, I see Kyla struggling to escape but the creature has locked her with its claw. There's no option. I run up to the bird and duck a swinging wing before placing the gun on its leg. As I pull the trigger I feel the blood and flesh of its leg explode around me and cover my face. Something's in my mouth. I don't investigate, just spit it out.

The creature is wheeling around, shrieking crazily. Kyla is hobbling and I grab her arm to wrap it round my shoulder. She shakes her head and points at the desk.

"We need something from that!"

I shake my head. "Go! We need to go!"

"I'll cover you," she yells.

"No! We need to go. I won't see you dead." I grab her hand this time and run for the door. She follows reluctantly, and I feel like I am pulling her. We hear the creature's wings clatter the door as we make it through. As we clear the outer room, Kyla shuts the door behind us. We have barely travelled a few yards when the door behind us explodes and the creature is upon us.

A wing slams Kyla against the side of the corridor and one of the grotesque paintings falls to the ground. I turn to face it but am butted by the creature and lift before falling onto my back. And it's over me so quickly that I can't roll away. A great clawed foot sits on top of my chest pinning me to the floor before I see the beak being lifted to peck down on me.

As the beak begins to descend a fist catches it on the side of the head pushing the beak sideways and it drills into my arm. I cry in pain. It's like a white hot pain I have never felt before. I see Kyla's figure ducking and weaving around the creature, delivering blow after blow which has little effect, but does manage to dislodge the claw holding me. I roll clear and try to get to my feet.

"Run, Mulgrew! I can't hold it for much longer."

I can't leave her. I can't! But there's nothing I can do. The creature is so strong. Nothing we have done has slowed it down at all. She's hitting it with blows that would have felled a prize fighter ten times over, but this bird just keeps coming.

"Run, Kyla! Just run, girl!"

"No! You can get out, Mulgrew. Go! Just go! I'll get you clear!"

There's a sweeping fear come over me. I can't lose her. I've only just found her. Dear God, no! Give me strength, give me something. Are you watching? You need to save her. I need you. I ain't got the strength. Please…

"Get out of the way!"

It's Gonzales.

"Step to the side of the wall, Boss!"

I immediately flatten myself to the wall side, and I watch him toss a gas canister down the corridor. It rolls past me, and I yell at Kyla. She's surprised and caught off balance allowing the bird to catch her across the face with a claw. There's blood dripping from her mouth and cheek, but she's upright and begins to run.

The canister bumps into the bird's leg causing it to stumble and fall onto its face. Gonzales has his firearm out and is shooting right past us. It's like I can feel the bullets passing me, they are so close. Kyla's hand grabs me by the collar, and we run past Gonzales who continues to fire.

"The damn bird's in the way. I can't hit the canister!" Kyla stops and turns around. I see the bird rise up again, ready to pursue us. Taking Gonzales' gun from his hands, Kyla drops to one knee and fires two rounds.

There's an almighty explosion and fire shoots along the corridor knocking me off my feet. There's a cry of "burn, you bastard!" from Kyla. I feel a fireball pass overhead and look for my team to be following me. Gonzales is running now and passes me. Then I see the glorious sight of Kyla in full flow. Her face is a mess of green and red blood, but I swear she has never seemed more beautiful.

"Stop gawking and go!" she yells at me. As we reach the ladder, I realise that Gonzales now has Hughes over his shoulder. His ascent up the ladder is remarkable, but then we don't know the bird is dead or even what it is?

Inside the pier hut, Gonzales pauses.

"We need a hospital!"

"No!" I yell. "We need to keep this under wraps or they will be after us. We go to Jenny Tatler. She'll know someone."

It's the middle of the night, and we are in the shadows as we run for our car. Kyla slips behind the wheel as Gonzales lies Hughes in the back seat before getting in and cradling her head. I fall into the passenger seat, and we speed off. The adrenalin starts to wear off despite the urgency of getting Hughes help.

Kyla's driving, but I can hear the sobs behind her breathing. She's barely holding it in, and no wonder after the fight she's just had.

"We're clear, Kyla. It's okay."

"Okay?" she yells back. "Hughes could be at death's door. I'm battered, and you're pretty wrecked too. And for what? Hughes could be dead for what?"

"We're out! That's what counts. Hughes will be good. What we needed doesn't matter."

"But now we don't even know where to look for them again. Shit, Mulgrew, Who knows what these bastards will unleash next?"

"Actually, we might know," says Gonzales.

"How? Just flaming how, Gonzales?" screams Kyla.

"Well, I ain't checked it but the paperwork from the drawer Hughes opened is inside my jacket. It might help."

"You son of a bitch, Gonzales," I say, "You are one fly mother!"

33

Chapter 33

"This isn't normal Trimble, and I don't like it!"

It's been a long time since I had a row with Jenny Tatler, but it seems it's finally come round. To be fair, we did pull up at her place demanding to know if she knew any medical specialists who would be prepared to go on the quiet to a woman who's clearly in dire need of help. I can feel the anger despite the quiet demeanour she is showing on the telephone with one of her contacts.

The phone is placed back in its cradle.

"Okay, she's coming. But she's also very spooked. You treat her right, Trimble, or I'll beat your sorry ass with the sharp end of a sword!"

"Okay," I say, waving my hands in a calming fashion. "I know this is irregular, but we need to focus on what's important. And thank you, Jenny, there's not many I would trust."

She gives a "humpf" and turns on her heel out of the room. There's a sound of taps running while I get some sharp looks from the others. I shake my shoulders in response.

"Leave Hughes on the sofa for the minute," says Jenny re-entering the room. "I'll check the rest of you over. Corstain, isn't it? You look a mess girl, I'll see you first. Then you, Trimble. And what's your name, Officer?"

"Gonzales."

"We'll, Officer Gonzales, the kitchen is in there. I drink coffee, black and strong. Trimble likes his a little weaker, unlike his women, and Corstain will have whatever after I've seen to her. Don't look for affirmation from him, son. You're in my house so haul ass and get the coffee sorted. I assume you've seen a kitchen before."

Gonzales lopes away like a scorned animal. I had forgotten how aggressive Jenny could be when she's pissed off. And my, is she pissed off. It could be the blood Kyla's been dripping onto the floor from her face. I really thought that it would have congealed by now.

Kyla walks past me and drops down to whisper in my ear.

"So you like strong women? Hope I can live up to her."

I want to say she doesn't need to. I want to say that she's gorgeous and sexy and like no one else. And I want to say I want her, no one else, and that she doesn't have to be anything. But she's away before I can reply.

Sitting, watching Jenny patch Kyla up, I think about Hughes. She's breathing but she hasn't moved. Who knows what sort of poison was on the dart that hit her? It's also been twenty minutes since Jenny got off the phone with her friend.

"Jenny, where is…"

"Shut it, Trimble. Just damn well shut it. You show up here demanding help, and now you're complaining. I'm working, so just shut it."

With that, there's a knock on the door. We all just sit there until Jenny pipes up, "As the only worker here, will someone else answer the bloody door?"

I get up, which is harder than I expected, as my muscles have tightened after tonight's exertions. Checking the spy-hole in the door, I see a rotund woman of maybe fifty. She doesn't appear armed but does seem nervous. I open the door.

"Hi, I'm…"

"Joyce, you came! Good girl! I'm busy working on Corstain here. You're problem is on the couch. Got hit by a needle with who knows what on it, and she's be breathing but not conscious since."

The lady shuffles in and I can see the spy hole did her a favour. She's very rotund and could do with dropping at least ten pounds if not double that. She gives me a sudden glance and her face looks like a rabbit in headlights.

"Who's these people?"

"Joyce, don't ask, okay? This is top secret police stuff, and I need your help because you're the best at this stuff. Don't fret on it, dear. I'll come over just as soon as I have finished these stitches on this woman's face."

"Okay, Jenny. This one is that guy from the photos you have."

"Yes, Joyce. That's the dumb ass clown that broke my heart because he couldn't handle a strong woman. If it was him, then I wouldn't have called."

I pull a face at Jenny. There's a scowl in return.

"It's like Jenny said, Joyce," I explain. "She was hit with a needle at close range, and since then she hasn't moved. But she's breathing." Joyce eyes me suspiciously.

"Where was the wound?"

"There, I believe."

"You believe?" queries Joyce.

"Yes, it was all a bit frantic in there."

"Where was that?"

"Joyce doesn't need to know that," harps Jenny.

Turning round to Jenny, I retort, "I know that. I damn well know that, Jenny, 'cause I'm a cop, and if she doesn't know then she doesn't get too deeply involved. I know how to protect secondary parties."

"But you didn't protect me!"

There's a silence and the truth of her anger finally dawns on me. It's Kyla's presence. Some year's ago, I told Jenny too much about a particular case, and she went snooping on her own and got herself kidnapped. They weren't pleasant with her, and she's had difficulties in the physicality department with relationships. She's propositioned me a few times on a late Friday night. But with Kyla here, she knows that will never happen. She's clicked on how close we have become.

"I'll take a look then, shall I?" says Joyce, breaking the silence.

Joyce breaks out a small briefcase and takes out a few phials and bottles of solutions. Gonzales is dispatched for more coffee, and for the next few hours, we wait and get patched up.

It's been four hours since Joyce began her investigations, and she seems to be becoming more frantic. From time to time, Jenny takes her aside and there are debates and frequent trips to the computer. Finally, it comes to a head as Joyce says out loud that "She has no friggin' idea as there's nothing there." With that, her case is packed inside of a minute, and she high tails it out of the house into the cool dawn light.

"What the hell was that, Jenny?" I ask.

"That was a very dear friend of mine pushed beyond her limits and whom I am going to have to spend some serious apology time with in order to keep her as a friend."

"Why? What's up?"

"She couldn't find anything. I pushed her and insisted on checking this and that. Everything came up negative. So I pushed again, told her she must be missing something. She's not used to this sort of pressure. She's usually in a lab, not on the pitch when it's game time. And she couldn't find anything."

"So she's missed something. We need to get someone else."

Jenny places her hands on her hips which is never a good sign. "No, Sherlock. It means there's nothing. Whatever is keeping Hughes like that, it isn't anything science knows anything about."

Looking at Hughes a dread comes over me. It's nothing science knows anything about. I need the priest, I need the priest. Where the hell is the priest?

Chapter 34

I grab Gonzales and tell him to get in the car. Hughes needs someone who understands these strange things, and the only person I know of is the priest. As he's not returning calls and hasn't been seen, then I'll go to his people.

I tell Kyla to get some rest and head to the front door. In the porch, Jenny grabs my arm and pulls me close.

"Are you serious with her?" I nod. "See when you get the bit between your teeth. That moment when you take the bull by the horns, that concern to get it sorted, *that* is what made me want you. And sometimes it still does. Stay safe."

Women so often pick the stupidest time for a personal moment. My head's full of possible locations of the priest, possible outcomes of his disappearance, many not good. And also of thoughts about Hughes, her family, what to do if it goes bad. And Jenny hits me with this. Kyla's not even getting much of a look in at the moment.

"I will." It sounded so corny. I want to give a quick salute and tell her to keep the breakfast warm as we'll only be a jiffy. But that's so often the truth. The deep and important moments come out corny at least six times out of ten. Or maybe that's just me.

Outside, I tell Gonzales to drive and get into the passenger seat. Jenny's staring out of the porch and Kyla's looking out the window. I really prefer women to come along one at a time as I have enough difficulty with them on their own, never mind together. Not that the single moments are an everyday occurrence.

"Where to, Boss?"

Gonzales' question snaps my mind back to the matter in hand. Where do I start when there's no clue as to his whereabouts?

"The cathedral, Gonzales. If he's not there, some of his people will be, and maybe they can be of use."

The car pulls out of Jenny's drive, and I ask Gonzales for the documents he pulled from the drawer in the underground chamber. He pulls from his jacket and apologises from not giving them over sooner, but he had had a look and the language written there was nothing he had ever seen in his life. He's right. There seems to be all manner of symbols and what looks like hieroglyphs along with some gruesome images.

"We'll see if any of the priest's people can decipher this," I tell Gonzales and settle into my seat for the short drive.

It's morning now, and the streets are filling up with commuters on their way in. After the chaos of previous days, it's astonishing how quickly people get back to their routine. I guess it shows stability. Gives them a crutch to lean on so they don't have to think about things. I sometimes wish my work was routine.

There's not much movement at the cathedral, and after parking we skirt around looking for a door. There's an open one at the rear of the cathedral, and we step inside, shouting out for some assistance. Shortly, a pleasant young woman approaches us and enquires after our business. She states that the priest is unavailable but says little else until I pull my badge on her.

"He's missing, Officer."

"Detective, Ma'am. How long has he been missing?"

"Nearly forty -eight hours."

"Have you reported it to the precinct?" Gonzales enquires.

"No." She turns to me. "Are you the one he was working with?"

"Yes, I'm Trimble."

"Where's the woman then? He said you were partnered with a woman."

"Ah," I say, "that's a bit of a long story. At the moment she's been injured and is also helping a colleague. In fact, we need your help. One of our colleagues has been incapacitated but not medically. It's a curse or something spiritual?"

I expect her to raise at least an eyebrow, but she seems non-plussed. Just a curt follow-me, and she turns on her heel. We pass along stone corridors which cut this way and that with little rooms off to the side. Without warning, she turns into one of these rooms and ushers us in. The basic wooden door is closed behind us, and I realise we are in a cell. Not a prison cell but a Nun's cell.

"This is Sister Martha. Sister, these are the people Father was working with before he disappeared. Detective, whilst Father has several deputies who can run the cathedral, Sister Martha is accomplished in the fields you require. I will leave you in her hands."

I look at the nun who has just been introduced. She's sitting, dressed in black and her face is covered by a veil.

"Which of you children is Trimble?" Her voice is croaky, and she coughs afterwards.

"I am." Although I'm not that keen on being called a child.

"Come to me." The nun is sitting on a small wooden bed. There's a table with a laptop and a glass of water. Otherwise, the cell is unfurnished.

I step over to the nun, and she coughs up some phlegm.

"Sit down on the bed, I need to see you." I sit and wait for her next move. Her wimple is shielding her face from me, but I see her hands and they are incredibly worn. She turns round to me, and I watch her hands rise up to my face and begin to explore. She traces the line of my nose, clutches at my cheek bones and ruffles my hair. Her hands are above her head, and I estimate she must be less than five foot tall.

"The priest is missing, and I need to find him."

"I know that," she says. "I also know who has him. But first, you have more important needs. Your friend Hughes needs help." I'm confused as to how she knows this, and I watch her head tilt back slowly, revealing first a toothless smile and then her nose. I watch her wimple lift past her eyes and then my jaw drops.

I swear she's looking at me, staring right at me. Although her face is scarred and dried by age it doesn't prepare me for what I see. This nun who I feel staring right into me has no eyes with which to see.

35

Chapter 35

Sister Martha rises to her feet and walks to the door. There's no hesitation, no fumbling. It's a calm and direct walk. At the door, she shouts out into the corridor for "Mandy". Dismissing the Barry Manilow tune that instantly comes into my head, I feel the urge to assist this elderly woman back to her bed, but she spins on a heel showing incredible alacrity for a her years and marches back to her former position.

"Yes, Sister?" The voice is young and very high. Mandy's a chubby girl of maybe sixteen with thick rimmed glasses. There appears to be no surprise in her demeanour at our being in the room.

"Get Sister Mary. These gentlemen have a friend in need of healing. Spiritual healing, probably a curse. Take Mr..., what is your friend's name, Mr. Trimble?"

"Gonzales, Sister. And it's Detective."

"Indeed. Mandy, take Mr Gonzales with you to show Sister Mary the way. *Detective* Trimble and I have some other work to do."

Gonzales gives me a glance, and I nod. He joins Mandy in the corridor, and I sit down on the bed with Sister Martha. She seems frail, the occasional bony point showing through her habit. I wonder just how much use she can be.

"Doubts are normal, Detective, but you really should not show it with your visage. Father Krystanovic is a good friend, and I guess you will be of help in your own way. However, we don't have time to sit." Sister Martha rises to her feet and extends an arm to the door. "Shall we go?"

"Of course," I reply, "but where?"

"To find a priest, Detective, before it's too late. Do you have a car with you?"

"I presume that Gonzales will have taken that."

"Of course. Never mind, we have a vehicle."

Despite having no eyes, Sister Martha walks at pace along the corridors of the cathedral and begins to descend several staircases until we arrive at a lighted car park under the cathedral. There are six cars parked there, some old, some new and one's a Ferrari.

"Wow!" I say, "The collection must be good on Sundays."

"Don't be annoying, Detective. In this line of service, you need all sorts of things. I can tell you like the Ferrari but something a little less ostentatious perhaps. Let's take the Dodge."

"Okay, but where are the keys?"

"In it, but it's okay, I'll drive."

I stop in disbelief. She's navigated the whole way perfectly to here but she is in her normal surrounds. To drive a car you need eyes. "Maybe better if I drive," I suggest.

"Yes, you're right. Would look a bit off a blind old crone like me driving you about. Good thinking, Detective."

It's like that was the only reason, the look of it. I mean she's blind. Doesn't she get that? Well, of course, she does, but she's not going to drive a car I'm in.

There's a spiralling climb out of the basement car park before we break out into the street. The Sister says nothing, so I take a right and continue straight ahead for a while. It then dawns on me I don't know where we are going.

"Sister, where to?"

"My dear Detective Trimble, I thought you knew."

"Err…no." I wouldn't have asked, would I? She must be simple.

"Well you have the document, don't you?"

"Which document?"

"The one recovered by… Hughes wasn't it? That's how she was injured."

How does she know that? Someone has a direct line to this woman.

"Yes, Detective, someone does. I work for Him, and He kindly gives me directions."

How did she hear that?

"A little less of the wonder, Detective. You have a document we need to read but that document is in a language we don't understand. So we need to go to the library and get a book that will help us translate it." Sister Martha breathes in deeply like my fumbling around is beginning to annoy her.

"I don't think the library will have…"

"Detective Trimble, kindly cut the chatter and drive me to the library. As to the contents of our library, I think you will be surprised at the collections it has outside of the main sections. Now drive and relax. We will have a long day ahead of us if we are to get the document translated and then find our mutual friend. Let us trust we are not too late."

Chastised, I settle back into my seat and drive. I'm heading the right direction. Until a few years ago, the city library was in the centre of town, but a great fire swept through the building. Fortunately, fire proofing had saved the important collections, and a new library was built on the outskirts of the city. And as I remember, it has a coffee outlet.

I pull into the wide car park that sits aside the impressive white building. There's a lake complete with swans surrounded by sculpted miniature hills. I race round to Sister Martha's side and hold the door open for her.

"Thank you, Detective, but there's really no need. I'm not an invalid."

"Indeed Sister, but there is the look of it to think about." Finally, a win in our conversation.

The Sister allows me to escort her inside the building, and we enter into a vast open space complete with cloakrooms and displays. I look at the signs for "languages" but feel my arm tugged in another direction. I comply, and we set off along the entrance hall until we stop in front of the coffee shop.

"This is a coffee shop, Sister. I doubt we're going to find anything of use in here."

"You like coffee, Detective. And we are going to be some time. You may find yourself here several times in the following hours. Get your coffee."

How does she know all this? It's like I've been profiled. "Can I get you anything?"

"Water. Make sure it's still. Not that fizzy nonsense."

"Yes, Sister."

"And, Detective, sub level 4, look for room 4.145. There's a lift. Don't spill the coffee."

With that, she turns and walks off. Well, damn the look of it then!

36

Chapter 36

"I walk with no eyes. You think I am weak, but I have a strength you haven't. And yes, you are right, it is crazy, but that's the way of it. Now you will have to go outside. Your thoughts are ringing through my head at a time when I need to concentrate. Pop back in in an hour and see if I need anything."

"So I'm meant to just hang about?"

"Yes. But why don't you ring that woman you treasure. And when you are talking, do remember to ask about your colleague. It would be good to know how they are getting on."

Dismissed, I think of making a show but there's no point. She is right. I am of little use. On I walk from the depths of the library up to the light outside and a cool breeze. Coffee in hand, I sit on a bollard and let my mind soak it all in.

It's going to be worse. We haven't seen the worst. Not for me to stop this demon. The Sister seems so aware of what's happening and yet I know so little.

My shoulders slump, and I feel a little pain across my back. Stress. Truly stress. Dear God, how do you deal with all this?

And then she's coming back into my mind. Kyla, she said ring Kyla. I pull out my mobile. There's a twinge of excitement as she answers the call.

The first three minutes of the call I spend listening to her voice. I don't hear any words just the tone of her voice. What am I like chasing after this young one? But she has a way of just lifting me by the merest sound of her. She could be chewing me out, and I'd still feel good.

"Mulgrew, did you hear what I said? They have Hughes lying on the floor, and there's ten of them now huddled over her praying. I'm waiting for the holy water. I ain't seen this before. We all pray, but not like this."

"Let them be, Kyla. I'm seeing things that just ain't normal here too. But they are working, and they seem to know what they are doing. Just keep everyone together, and try to get some rest. I think this is all going to change soon. I'm sure you're scared, I know I am."

I put the mobile away in my pocket and stare again at the people moving about in the car park. It seems surreal knowing everything that is going on and watching the uninhibited daily wanderings of the people. I see a young kid toddle about. The Chief would have said that's who we do it for so that they can be safe and free of worry. Of course, that was before he tried to have me killed and then put a gun to his head.

There's a pain coming right into my forehead. It's like a jackhammer has been placed on it and is pounding away. And then a face appears. It's old and has no eyes. I recognise her wimple. But it's a face that's battered around its sightless eyes. There's blood pouring from it. But then another face replaces it causing me to scream out loud. I drop my coffee and it splashes out of the cup across the ground. But I only hear that as I am running with everything I have to get to Sister Martha.

Chapter 37

I race past confused people wondering where this mad man is going. There's a bin to hurdle and then steps to concentrate on as I try to take them two at a time. It's easier going up than down and I nearly lose it altogether on a couple of occasions. There's still a pounding in my head, and I just know something is wrong. Reaching the corridor of the room, I see the door explode off its hinges and fly across the empty passageway. What on earth is going on in there?

A moment later, I'm turning into the room, and I see Sister Martha up against the wall. Beneath her a long knife lies on the ground. Something is pinning her to the wall but I can't see anything. She sees me and begins to shout.

"Get out. Just get out. You don't know what's in here."

She's got me there. But I enter and try to grab the knife on the ground. Something hits me hard in my stomach causing me to nearly retch. My leg is grabbed by something, and I am flung across the room, crashing into the wall.

"He will come!"

It's a harsh and dark sounding voice that reaches into your

head. I'm not sure it was spoken but rather implanted into my consciousness. But it's not aimed at me.

"Be gone, fiend! Murderer! Leave this place." Sister Martha struggles to maintain the strength of her voice as if she is being choked. Realising she is under serious threat, I raise myself onto my hands and look towards her.

There's a faint outline, a bit like the air around the steam from a kettle. There's motion but very indistinct. But all the motion is around Sister Martha. Her body moves up the wall, arms outstretched like she is on a cross before she starts to turn. If she had eyes, I'm sure they would be wide and white in terror. Her face begins to tighten, the flesh drawn over the bones. Faint at first, lines emerge where the skin begins to break, dark red in colour. Blood then begins to pour from these increasing cracks.

I launch myself across the room and dive onto the knife on the ground. I hear movement behind me and don't wait but slash out to my rear. There's a small howl before my leg is grabbed again, and I am flung back across the room. The wall comes suddenly, and it's everything I can do to hold onto the knife.

"Fool! Is he one of yours? Does he not know what horrors I can bestow on him?"

My head is grabbed my two invisible hands. Or they may be claws or talons as there are pointed tips which scratch and cut into me. I feel myself being lifted up, and when I open my eyes, there is just blackness.

"What do you hold dear? What prize does your head contain?"

I feel helpless to resist, and I feel a rush of air passing me by. It's as if I am being lifted to somewhere high. And then light floods into my eyes causing me to blink. There's a number of tall buildings around me. And looking down, I see a familiar car park. It belongs to the cathedral, St. Luke's. Below there are people carrying a coffin. There's police in abundance and a guard of honour for it.

"This is your future. But I can give you something else. I can give you what you love. My head moves by someone else's accord, and I am shown the whole city around me. There's streets that I walked as a trainee cop years ago, places where I have seen rescues and killings, the bright lights of theatres and concerts combined with the squalor of brothels and crack houses. It's all there.

"Join me. Worship me, and I'll give you this. I'll make you Mayor of this place to govern and control."

There's robes around my body now. I look like a Mayor from England with all its pomp and ceremony. A three cornered hat on my head and a chain of office around me.

"Worship me and have all this."

We glide down to the city hall, and there are thousands of people cheering and waving amongst the ticker tape. I see a black limousine. Kyla wears an elegant but revealing dress and immediately kisses me on the cheek.

We walk along the line of cheering onlookers. There's police officers I know and other people from various coffee shops and places I frequent. They are all cheering. And then a little girl is standing in front of me with a large bunch of flowers obscuring her face. At this point I can see how to rule this city. I could finally bring this place to heel, to be a place for families and good, decent people.

The blonde woman with me takes the flowers from the girl who then turns towards me. The child is perfect in form with her brown hair and chubby cheeks. But she has no eyes. They are just closed over with scars. And the child speaks.

"Who are you to govern?" It's Sister Martha's voice!

And I'm whisked away to a beach. I'm stood on perfect white sand with a crashing sea to my right. The salt air tastes good, and there's a warm sun tempered by a steady breeze.

"Mulgrew, come here!"

It's Kyla. I spin round to see her in the sand. She's crawling along by her hands, her legs seemingly not functioning. She's dressed in just a pair of bikini bottoms but her back is scarred with lashes. She looks up, and I see her jaw is smashed in. Her nose is clearly broken and blood is pouring from it.

I feel the anger rising up in me. There's a building rage that grows with every glance at my love.

"Or you can save her. Worship me!"

Another Kyla is now beside the one on the ground. She's dressed the same, but her body resonates with the beauty of the beach. There's hunger in her eyes, and I see what she should be.

"You can save her."

I look again, and her eyes are now gone, replaced with great scars.

"Why would you control her? Choose her path for her. Do that, and she'll never be a woman to stand beside you. He lies!"

I look down and there is the knife in my hand. Gripping it tight I look around and see the slight change in the air. That shimmer. I plunge the knife into the discrepancy.

38

Chapter 38

The image goes and I'm back in the library room. The knife is in my hands still, and I'm slashing hard at something in front of me. Sister Martha is still upside down, arms outstretched, and pinned to the wall. My attacks at the invisible in front of me get wilder, but I can feel them reaching something. And then Martha drops off the wall.

I instinctively try to run to her but get caught by an invisible limb that throws me across the room again. My ribs are screaming at me as I land, and I'm struggling to get back up. Something grabs me by the back of the neck, lifting me off my feet.

"Holy woman, you filth, time to watch him die!"

I try to get a purchase on something to attack the creature with but nothing comes to hand. I can feel another claw close on my throat and begin to choke. There's a hot breath on my neck, and I smell something foul. I'm waiting for my neck to be snapped and a panic races around my body.

"Not today, envoy. Too many have died at your hand. It's time to send you back to the darkness!"

Martha has stood up and has her face pointed our direction. There's no eyes, and she looks a shocking sight, but to me at this moment she might just be an angel. There's a small curl to her lips, a hint of a smile, the first I have seen on her face. A knife emerges from her habit, flying towards me. It rushes past my neck, and I feel my neck being freed. I fall to the ground.

Sister Martha is across the room at a pace too fast for her age. From beneath her habit, she kicks out at the invisible being behind me, pushing me to one side. Her legs are bare and have the outer signs of age on them, blue veins showing, scars and scabs. But each leg is also toned and strong.

The kicks come one after the other before she picks up her knife and the one I dropped. She now fights like a Sai-wielding martial artist. Her moves are a blur, but I repeatedly watch her smile as she connects, I assume, with our attacker. At one point she is struck, and her wimple falls to the ground and long grey hair flows from her head. A few more efforts and she stops. Her face turns to me and there's a smile.

"He won't be bothering us again. Unfortunately, I don't think he's the main problem."

"Who the hell are you?" I ask.

"Your friend. I guess that's lucky for you." She laughs out loud, and I watch her place the knives back inside her habit before placing her wimple back on her head. "Are you okay, Detective?"

"No Sister, I am not."

"And Detective, I have nothing to do with hell, unlike the envoy which I have just dispatched back to its own realm."

"Envoy?"

"The creature that has been killing people, seemingly without leaving any marks. And the one that let you live. It could have killed you without even trying and yet you are still here. He wanted you for his own to control."

I try to shake the pain out of my head. Everything hurts, but my head is winning in the truly buggered stakes. "He showed me the city. Offered me a Mayorship. Then he offered me Kyla."

"I know. You may remember I was there."

"Yes. In all sorts of faces. How do you do that?"

"It's a gift. Sometimes I think I lost something when my eyes were taken, but I was given so much more. Pain can be a gift, but it can also be a destroyer. You'll need to remember that."

She turns away from me at this point, and I feel her pity for me. "What's that meant to mean?"

"As I said to you in the visions. Don't hold too close to that which is dear to you for it won't grow, develop and be what it should be. But to let something grow sometimes means you have to take the pain of their struggles to get there."

"You mean Kyla."

"Kyla, this city, everyone. We're not God, and He doesn't even do it. So neither should we."

At this point I usually retreat to a coffee cup for solace and reflection. The room is a mess, and my ribs hurt as I try to move.

"Get up! We need to tidy this room and then leave for somewhere else to look at these documents. They must have realised you took them and then sent the envoy after them. It can follow things in a way us humans can't. But once they realise it's gone, they will follow in cars. These documents are important, important enough to risk their envoy. Come on Detective, get up!"

I try, but my ribs are on fire. "Sorry, but I can't. My ribs are soo sore. I think a few are cracked."

"We can't have that, Detective." She steps forward and bends down to me, pushing my shirt up and exposing my ribs. I murmur in pain, trying to stifle a loud cry, and I hear her start to pray. Some words I understand, some I don't. She stays kneeling over me for at least five minutes.

"Get up, Detective, let's get going."

"But I can't…" Sister Martha grabs my arm and hauls me to my feet. I try to steady myself, ready for the pain that my ribs will unleash on me, but there's nothing. I twist left and right and there's nothing.

"Don't stand there and gawp, Detective, it always seems a bit disrespectful to me. Have a bit of faith. Your wounds are healed, so let's not look back but get on. Say thanks but move on."

"Thank you!"

"Not to me! To Him." There's a smile on her lips again, and I wonder just what else there is to her.

39

Chapter 39

I still don't know how she blagged her way past the library attendant who was mighty confused by the noise that had come from the room, or who had acquiesced to letting the reference only books, and mighty expensive ones at that, out of the building. Sister Martha, weak, innocent and blind was proving to be quite a surprise.

We took to the car again and headed out of the city towards the national park on the outskirts. My mother had a cabin up there, which while nothing special, my sister has kept on, and I reckon it should be an out of the way place to get work done on these documents.

Sister Martha seems relieved as we drive along, and has the odd page of the documents on her lap. Despite having no eyes, her head is pointed out the window whilst her hands are gently moving back and forth across the pages. There's no braille imprints, just the marks left by the ink, but she's reading them all the same. I am glad she's on our side.

Time was when I would be sitting in the back of a Dad's big Ford and annoying my sister with gentle flicks of the ear and punches to her arm. She'd moan to Mum about how annoying I was, but secretly we both would be looking forward to getting to the cabin and then swimming in the lake. I think about taking Kyla here and swimming but not in so innocent a pursuit as in my younger days.

There's tall trees as we enter the park, the sun filtering through the leaves and causing a dancing shadow as I drive. The path is proper asphalt for a while but then I break onto a stone path before a muddier option presents itself.

The small log cabin has its shutters down and doesn't look inviting, but I tell Sister Martha how good it looks. Who am I kidding? The woman sees better than me. She stands and looks out across the lake. Well she points her face that way. I just can't get used to the idea of her seeing with no eyes. All my life I have dealt with the darker side of humanity, but everything was at least understandable. Dark but normal. Now it's all bizarre, even the good side.

I throw up the shutters while Martha spreads the documents out on a basic table in the kitchen. The cabin has three bedrooms, small but adequate, as well as a living room and a kitchen. Unfortunately, my sister is a philistine when it comes to coffee, and I have to offer the Sister instant.

"Thank you, Detective. I'm sorry but I would ask you to now leave me in peace again. The languages these documents are written in take a lot of concentration, and I fear you would break my thoughts."

"As you wish," I reply. "I'll just be outside not disturbing anyone."

The Sister glances up with a smile before looking down at her work. I know, she doesn't look technically, but she still makes the heads motions. It's easier to think she's looking.

Sometimes you have to make the weird normal.

Outside the cabin, I take a walk towards a small lake, one where we used to swim as kids. It seems strange seeing the places you grew up with, places that have barely changed. The city's changed. You see technology bringing in new things all of the time, but out here, there's something almost timeless. Except those trees are a damn sight larger.

Technology buzzes in my pocket, and I check my mobile. The temporary Chief has been trying to contact me. No doubt about the library incident. I decide not to contact back until I have some idea of what we are going to do. I sit down on the grass by the pool and then lie back onto the ground, just because I can. There are a few clouds drifting by the tree tops, and I stare at them, happy to just be doing something that's nothing. No killing, no fighting, no demons, no strangeness.

I feel a chill across my back. The lights dimmed somewhat, maybe a cloud is passing by. No, the sun's lower, I must have fallen asleep. My head's sore, probably from the lack of sleep and that the recent kip is not enough. I check my watch and notice it's almost five. Time to see if the Sister has anything. And to get some food.

She's still got her hands on documents when I come into the cabin, but the smile I left her with is gone. There's a concern on her face that is drawing me in but I'm reticent to ask any question lest I disturb her.

"It's okay, you disturbed me when you came in."

"Sorry," I say, "but I fell asleep and was just wanting to see if you needed any food."

"Thank you. What do we have?"

I hadn't thought of this and start to raid the cabin's cupboards for supplies. Well, there's soup or soup. Tinned soup, mind.

"Chicken or tomato?" I ask, holding the options in either hand.

"Chicken. Best to get some meat into you."

"Well, I wouldn't get your hopes up, this is a budget tin."

I warm the soup up in a pan whilst the Sister continues her work but she starts to mutter to herself. It becomes disconcerting when she almost chants. She must be reading aloud the texts because the language she's using is unrecognisable to me. She slams her fist to the table. And again.

"Are you okay, Sister?"

No response.

"I asked if you are okay."

"Yes, I am. Shush!"

The soup is becoming ready when she starts thumping the table again. I think about interrupting but then think better of it. She becomes frantic, tearing herself from one document to another. There's a scream of frustration, then a word totally foreign, then an exclamation of delight. She stands and begins to pace the floor. Then, without warning, she turns to me.

"Soup ready?"

"Yes."

"Well then, pour us both some and sit down."

I do as asked, and I sit opposite her at the table. Taking the steaming hot cup of soup she sips it gently. Eyes are the windows to the soul, and their exclusion makes a person hard to read. But she's worried. There's just the slightest showing of worry.

"What's bothering you, Sister?"

"Detective, how much do you know about bombs?"

40

Chapter 40

"What do you mean bombs?"

Her face turns my way and creases up in a confused expression. Without the eyes, it's been hard to tell if she is kidding me. "The exploding kind, Detective. Are you aware of any other?"

I grab my mug and sip some soup. "How many? Where? When? What's the target?"

"Easy, Detective. I shall explain as best I know. As you know, there is a "Darkness" coming. It seems that our friends wish to welcome it in with a grand sacrifice. Rather than kidnap and line up some thousands of people, the preferred method is to explode them."

"But where?"

"Several places. There is a pattern to the explosions. At least a twisted logic. The first place is the Catholic cathedral, during mass, I believe. There is a visiting priest, no bishop, I believe. There will be a full cathedral, all ripe to be massacred. It describes a purging by fire."

"Okay, so that's an easy one to find," I say. "Where else?"

"The main stadium, on the city outskirts. This says a purging by water."

"Okay, not sure how they'll do that. And what's it got to do with bombs?"

"Explosion is the method. Explosion leading to drowning."

I nod but have no idea how this is to occur. "What else?"

"The docks. A laying waste of the foreigner. This one is extremely difficult to decipher. I don't know the how, but there is a mention of bombs again."

"Okay, and the last one?"

"The last one speaks of a fog which kills. Somewhere in the industrial area, a destruction of commerce."

"And that's all we have? Nothing more specific."

"Only that it's all happening at midnight tonight, which I make it as less than seven hours." There are deep lines of worry across her face. And she's shaking slightly.

"Drink up your soup, we need to get going. We'll get to the station, and you can tell my boss everything. It'll take some manpower to cover those areas."

"You'll drop me back at my cell. I have preparations to make."

I give her an incredulous look. "No way, lady. You are the only expert I have on this. I need you with me on this. You need to work on giving me some more detail."

"The detail is that there will be a "Darkness" arriving in this town that needs to be met with force in order to put it back where it should be. I cannot afford to mess about but shall instead assemble a team to confront the "Darkness" when it arrives."

"Do you want back-up for that? Police, military, ambulances?"

She laughs, raucously. "Detective, I would not endanger

these people, wonderful as they are in what they do for this world. I require something special."

"So, we just leave you to it?"

"Yes. You have four threats to deal with before midnight. Understand that this will be destruction on a grand scale for this is a welcome to their master. If I succeed, it will be a hollow victory surrounded by mass bodies. Protect the public, Detective. Do your job. Let me do mine."

I nod and walk out of the cabin. Calling the station, I ask the desk sergeant to call in everyone he can who isn't already at work, giving the major incident password. I also ask him to get the new Chief to meet me in half an hour in the main conference room at the station.

Kyla's my next call, and I am relieved to hear that Hughes is improving. She's shocked at the detail I give but agrees to meet at the station with Gonzales.

I get a shock as Martha tells me to get into the passenger seat so that she can drive. The car wheels spin as she places the vehicle into drive, and we hurtle down the track back to the main roads. Disconcerting is not the word, as my eyeless friend throws the car around at speeds I wouldn't comprehend. As we reach the major routes, we pick up a couple of tails from my police colleagues.

I ask Martha to allow them to get alongside us so I can flash my badge, but instead she races off, leaving them in our wake, citing a lack of time. I swear, she's only just becoming alive.

The car breaks to a halt outside the station, and I get out quickly, part of me worried she'll pull away with my leg still inside the car.

But instead, she leans across and shouts at me.

"Stop those bombs. Whatever it takes! This "Darkness" will

grow from the destruction, it will feed on it. If I can't stop it, then it needs to be kept reduced. Whatever it takes, Trimble! Whatever!"

And she's gone. Cars dive out of the way as she dominates the road. Well, I can't wait around for that. Inside the station, I climb the stairs two at a time until a hand reaches out and stops me.

"Mulgrew! He's ready for you, but he's going to need some convincing." Kyla's stood in her black jeans and leather jacket and looks like she hasn't slept in a few days. There's a face that defines worry and eyes begging for some hope. But damn she still looks stunning.

I grab her and pull her close. I press against her lips and feel them part and we enjoy each other briefly. "When this is done, I have something to ask you."

"If we get this done. If we're both here."

"When. Come with me, I'll need you in with me. He needs to understand what we're up against."

"And do you know?"

I stop in my tracks. "No. But the Sister does. And I know what we need to do. So let's do it."

Reaching the conference room, I notice the hubbub of noise in the surrounding offices. There's a lot of officers about. Good. He didn't stop them coming in. One small victory, let's get another. I'm about to open the door when Kyla grabs my shoulder.

"Mulgrew, there's something close. I can feel it. Kyla clutches her head. "Be careful in there."

I kiss her forehead and open the door. At the far end of the table is the temporary Chief. Beside him, with her back to us, is a red-headed woman. She has smooth legs which follow curves up to her hips. A real femme fatale as far as I can see. Then she turns, and I see cherry red lips and a pale face. Her hair swings away from her face, and she looks at me. I remember those eyes. This woman tried to kill me. She fled from the beach.

"You!" I yell.

"Ah, good, Trimble," says the Chief, "You've met the Intelligence agency's local director. She's desperate to hear what you have uncovered."

41

Chapter 41

My mind's racing. I wasn't expecting this. I knew there were possibly people in high places, but she's with the Feds and she's one of them too. Dammit, she nearly killed me. And those eyes are staring, piercing, trying to find out what I know. How do I play this? After making a fuss, I can hardly just say there's nothing in front of her. I need to downscale it somehow. Give them something to investigate that she can't get away from.

"There's going to be an attack tonight at the game. Tonight's Whalers game is going to be attacked, Chief, bomb threat."

And where does this information come from?" She runs her tongue quickly across her lips after the question believing that I'll give up my source. How much do I know, that's what she's asking.

"Informant confirms what I've learnt from documents seized from this group, Chief."

"And who is this informant?" Again she presses.

"Yes Trimble, who is it?" encourages the Chief.

"Can't say, boss. They are still deep in and may be instrumental in resolving this, so I don't want to blow their cover."

"It can stay within this room," says the woman, mentally surrounding me.

"No, it can't."

"Trimble, who is it?" asks the Chief.

"I'm not prepared to say, boss. I'm not saying you are involved, but given that my last superior was in cahoots and then tried to have me killed, I'd rather not expose my sources at this time with all due respect to yourself and our friend."

The Chief nods. My heart stops beating wildly, and inside I give a wild cheer and a metaphorical tongue is stuck out at the woman across from me.

"What time is the threat?" asks the Chief.

"I don't know," I lie. "But it is tonight."

"Well, given the importance of tonight's game, I doubt we can get it cancelled. The Mayor will say how it's a way of everything getting back to normal, so we'll have to manage the threat." The Chief looks out the window considering something. "Okay, I'll run point on this. Trimble, I want you to get back into the underbelly of this and find me who's doing this. I'll increase the security at the game and deploy a lot more cover. We'll get the dog teams and bomb squad down there. It's pretty thin information to go on, so get me some more, Trimble."

"Yes, sir, I'll leave you to organise and see what I can get hold of." I feel Kyla tap my hand, but I ignore her and turn on my heel to leave the room.

"Oh, Detective." It's the woman again. "Don't forget to pass on any more information. I can help you end this. Our entire resources will be put behind your intel."

"That's much appreciated. I'll be sure to let you know." I

nod at Kyla to follow me and walk off. In the corridor, Kyla taps my shoulder, but I tell her to wait until we reach the lift. The doors close, and her face looks confused.

"What are you doing? We've got four potential bomb threats! Why didn't you tell him the rest?"

"Because that woman tried to kill me on the beach when I exited the Saunderson. She was there. If I tell them what we know, who knows how much she'll obstruct it all so I had to give them one thing we knew. The game's so public that the Chief will have to cover it off."

"But the attack's at midnight, the game will be done and dusted by then. It's the one bit that doesn't make sense."

"I know, so best the resources are there. We're on our own with the others. The cathedral is friendly territory though, and we have friends who can influence things there for us. The foreigner bit I am clueless about. As for the industrial bit, there's a number of choices. There's not many people we can trust, so we'll need to split up. Is Gonzales here?"

Kyla nods. "But Hughes is out of the picture. How about Jenny Tatler? Or is there anyone else?"

"Jenny's a good call. And our other pathologist friend. That gives us five and a little bit of back-up. Okay let's round them up and meet for a plan. It's not a lot, but it's what we know to be safe. Sister Martha is going to confront this "Darkness" when it arrives."

"The blind nun?" asks Kyla.

"Kyla, she drives a car, she reads print with her hands and she fights better than you. She's one mean mother."

"Sister, she's just a sister."

"Let's get moving. Twenty minutes but not here. My coffee house, we meet there."

"Mulgrew?"

"Yeah."

Kyla grabs the back of my neck and drives her mouth into mine. Her hands briefly roam my torso before she breaks off. Stepping back she stares at me as the doors of the lift slide open. "You have something to ask me. So make sure you don't die out there."

I watch her walk out of the lift, her ass in her tight jeans swaying like the long hair dangling around her neck. Sometimes I feel old, my body creaks and cracks. Sometimes I have a weariness of having seen too much, too many bodies and too many broken lives. But right now, I could take on hell itself and royally kick its ass.

42

Chapter 42

We're thinly spread, and it seems like there's not enough of us. I'm taking the Chief on trust that he means to sort this out, but he might be hamstrung with that woman alongside him for the ride. At least the stadium should be fairly empty by midnight, in fact, most people would expect to be gone by an hour before midnight. Kinda scuppers their plans.

The planning at the coffee house wasn't exactly all fun and games either, Jenny Tatler being a serious obstruction. She was ready to take all this to the Chief and call in the Feds but that wouldn't have worked. It might even have accelerated their plans. At the moment they don't know what we know. The documents might have been burnt up in the fire at the pier. This ignorance of theirs to what we know is all I have going for me at the moment, and I ain't about to give it up.

I sent Jenny with Kyla to the docks to see if they can solve the riddle of the foreigner. She's no fighter, Jenny, but her brain is very sharp and she knows how to investigate. And Kyla will look after her.

Gonzales went to the cathedral. There's plenty of friendly faces for him to work with there. He's a good kid, but he doesn't have a lot of experience. At least the catholic priest will take him seriously. Which leaves me and my rather disbelieving forensic investigator to take the industrial area. I don't do all the processes and factory workings but he does. I'll need his eyes and thoughts.

O'Halloran is driving the car, which pisses him off immensely, but with all I've been doing, I can't focus with the simple.

"So how would you cause an explosion to welcome in a demonic entity, O'Halloran?"

"What sort of a question is that? Be serious."

"I am."

He dips his head slightly, eyes barely maintaining the road. "I don't hold with all this nonsense, there will be a reasonable explanation. I agree something dangerous is at work, some madman, but your hellfire ideas are too much."

"I ain't going to waste time arguing, instead we need to cover ground quickly. How would you kill the most people?"

O'Halloran sniffs. "I wouldn't do it, personally, but an explosion seems a bit strange. You would be better getting something airborne and able to reach over the city. The prevailing winds come across the industrial zone and blow away from the city which knocks that theory on the head."

"What way is the wind blowing tonight?"

"Actually, it is moving back across the city just now. That's quite unusual for this time of year."

"These people are somewhat unusual. How would you get something airborne?"

He thinks for a moment. "Something gaseous. Something

that would release upwards, a light gas escaping or created. And whatever you want to drop on the people entrained into that. Once it had gone up, you couldn't contain it."

"Okay, what factories? Then we'll need to do a search of the premises and itineraries. Multichem has an enormous gas storage unit, but the gas is fairly inert. Put something in it, though, and it would release high."

I look out at a passing vent from one of the factories passing us. The night is dark, but the lights from the buildings light up the steam coming from this vent. I say steam but really I haven't a clue what it is, but what is obvious, is that the vapour is moving upwards and then plateauing and even beginning to descend before it disappears. I point it out to O'Halloran.

"Damn, Trimble. That's an inversion. The conditions aren't right for that."

"Inversion?"

"Yes, a meteorological phenomenon but the conditions are all wrong, how the hell is that happening?"

"Hell's the right word. How long until we reach one of our suspect companies?"

"They ain't suspect. These are reputable companies. Multichem is up ahead."

O'Halloran pulls the car up to the gate, and a young man in a security outfit stops us. I pull my badge and ask to see the plant. He says that there's a deep clean team on site and that we can't get in. I cast a glance at O'Halloran who nods that this is normal.

"We need to see shipments in for the last week, son," I say, and to his credit, the guard calls someone on his radio. We are informed that a manager will be here shortly.

The factory is lit up quite spectacularly, and I see how some people see beauty in these places. Certainly, they look better at night. A car pulls up, and we are told to follow. Shortly after, we arrive at a management block.

I let O'Halloran take the lead and try to snoop around. The manager, a short man with wiry glasses, keeps a beady eye on me, but I get the feeling he's not the only one watching. It's now almost nine o'clock, and I'm beginning to get worried.

After what seems a thorough check, O'Halloran calls me over. "Everything seems okay, Trimble, nothing suspicious. We should get over to DynoForce."

"Agreed," I say, but there's something bothering me. "Do all of these places smell like this?"

"No point asking me with my sinuses, Trimble. I couldn't smell a curry from five feet. What are you smelling?"

"A musky smell. Sweaty, quite raw."

"Well the arm pits on that manager look damp. Probably that."

I nod, and we head back to the car. As O'Halloran steps to the car, he swears.

"What's up?"

"Dog shit, Trimble. Bloody dog mess." He wipes his foot on the ground, and I tell him to hurry up. We give our thanks to the manager and drive off towards DynoForce. As we pass along the industrial estates, there's a powerful stench in the car.

"Do your sinuses smell that, O'Halloran?"

"Pretty rank, must be the dog dirt still on my shoe."

"Pull over and then give me your shoe."

O'Halloran does as asked, but has a bemused look on his face. "I can clean it off myself."

I take the shoe and hold it under my nose, sniffing hard. It nearly makes me vomit from the harsh smell.

"Trimble, that's gross."

"How good are you on excrement?"

"Well, it's not a speciality. That's disgusting Trimble. You can't eat it."

It is disgusting, and I feel like I should vomit. "O'Halloran, I have walked this city for years and I've seen my fair share of dog shit, human shit and other animal shit. But I ain't ever smelt this. This is something else!"

43

Chapter 43

"What do you mean? You're trying to tell me that this faeces is not normal? It's otherworldly? Are you off your rocker? We're looking for bombs and explosives, Trimble."

"Turn the car around! There's something back there."

O'Halloran looks hard at me, and then shakes his head before turning the wheel. I tell him to cruise up to the perimeter.

"So what do we do Trimble? Just bust in? Walk in with our badge and announce the alien poo has arrived?"

"Shut up, O'Halloran. We go in via the fence and get close to where that shit came from. Remember there's a clean up on, mighty convenient."

Getting out of the car, I take the bolt cutters from the trunk and proceed to cut a hole in the wire fence. O'Halloran is jumping from foot to foot, nervous as anything.

"What's up, O'Halloran? You never bent the rules a bit."

"I'm a forensic investigator, not a cowboy, Trimble. We're going to end up in the mire with this one."

"Not if I can help it," I say returning the cutters to the trunk, the hole now complete. "When did you last hold a weapon?"

"I ain't taking a weapon."

"Your funeral, O'Halloran," I say taking a shotgun from the trunk. I make sure my handgun is also available to me. "Here, take this," I say offering O'Halloran a small side arm. At first he refuses, but then I force the weapon upon him.

"What are you expecting, Trimble?"

"I don't know, and you don't want to know."

Keeping to the shadows is no easy task as the complex is well lit with large floodlights. But there are corners of darkness, and I lead O'Halloran along these routes as we head back to where our car had been parked earlier. The air has the musky tinge to it I smelt earlier. We round a corner and O'Halloran gasps.

"What is it?"

"There, Trimble, just beyond the light. That's a body. At least what's left of it. Looks like it's been tossed about, chewed, attacked."

"And there's a uniform on it. We're in the right place, O'Halloran, and these guards don't know it. They have left something else to protect their secret."

A radio on the body squawks into life asking for a report. But there's no reply. There's another station called before the radio goes quiet mid-sentence. I look at O'Halloran and can see he's shaking. Poor guy doesn't get into the field like this very often.

I motion for him to withdraw his gun and keep his eyes open. Staying in the shadows, I make my way to the body we've seen, O'Halloran following behind.

"He's been ripped into by teeth. Canine in nature, but bigger than anything I've ever seen." O'Halloran is physically trembling as he says these things. He's a pathologist, a forensics expert who has seen many dead bodies, but I guess what killed them was never in the vicinity.

"Just breathe, O'Halloran. Just breathe and focus on what we need to do."

He nods, and I ask where the largest gas tank is. With a flick of the wrist, he indicates the way, and we remain in the shadows as we go along. The musky smell is everywhere, and at one point we stumble upon urine splattered around a pipe.

"It's marking territory," says O'Halloran. "It'll be back this way."

"Come on, no time to waste then."

Within minutes we can see the vast vessel which O'Halloran says is holding the light gas. I can't understand the name with its hexos and many numbers, but according to O'Halloran, it will rise up until it hits the inversion layer. At that point it will blow towards the city centre eventually descending.

We sneak close to the vessel and can see packages strapped to it. We both recognise explosives but it's pretty pointless blowing a harmless gas up into the air.

"Trimble, over there. Can you see the metal case?"

I nod and motion for O'Halloran to investigate. The large vessel looms over us and it's hard of O'Halloran to hold to the shadows as he moves for the case. For a moment he emerges into the light and then bends down to inspect the case. But behind him, there's something—sleek, black and with some sort of fur. And two eyes. Hunting eyes.

I empty both cartridges from the shotgun at the shadow that leaps towards O'Halloran. The shadow is thrown out into the light and I see some sort of large wolf, larger than a man, claws and teeth displayed, blood staining both. Green liquid is emerging from where my shots have struck the creature, but it is rounding onto its feet.

O'Halloran has collapsed to the ground, shaking. He's oblivious to the creature coming back to him.

Draw your weapon, you ass. Defend yourself!

Dropping another couple of cartridges into the chamber, I run towards the beast as it seizes O'Halloran by the foot. With its mouth, it tries to drag him away, but I hit it with both barrels again, knocking it aside, but it continues to hold O'Halloran.

The handgun is out of my pocket, the shotgun dropped, and I fire more shots into the creature.

Damn it, go down, go down!

44

Chapter 44

O'Halloran is screaming as he's dragged backwards. I continue to fire every round out of my handheld, but the creature seems able to continue despite the green splurging from its body. Its eyes are a pale orange, constantly on me, as its drags O'Halloran away. Although strong, it takes quite an effort to move O'Halloran, and I am gaining ground rapidly.

Drawing nearer, I see the beast loose its grip on the forensics expert and focus on me. It rushes forward and makes a leap for my throat. I turn as it reaches, allowing me to wrap an arm around its throat and then onto its back removing the threat of its claws for a moment.

The beast thrashes wildly, and I am holding on for dear life. My coat flaps around, and a claw rips a hole in it. The creature rolls over onto its feet and begins to shake me. My grip loosens, and I am thrown to the floor in front of the beast. Desperately, I look around for any sort of weapon. There's nothing. Just some loose grit.

It leaps again, and I drive forward, planting an open palm

into each eye, driving the grit in my hand deep into the eye sockets. Its claws envelope me, and I feel it rake my back. Green blood sprays across my face, and I am blinded for a moment. There's a thump and the claws release.

Wiping my face, I look around and see a limping O'Halloran. He's holding a piece of metal piping and is wincing as he tries to put his foot down. The creature is growling and looking around. From the wildness of its glances, it must be struggling to see, and I run over to O'Halloran and grab the piping. Approaching the beast from behind, I drive the piping into its back, missing its spinal bone and then hearing the pipe contacting the concrete below.

"Dear God, what is that?" asks O'Halloran.

"I don't know, but we need to get the bomb squad here to sort out these packages. I should take a look at your foot too."

"Never. Go and get back-up, I'll check my foot myself. I don't want some barbarian looking at it."

I laugh at the insult. He must be okay then. There's also a need to warn the others that there may be other elements in play other than the bombs and to be careful. I run back to the car and call up the station looking for the Chief.

"Trimble? Where are you? At the stadium?"

"Negative, sir, I'm in the industrial area at Multichem. There's been an incident here and a shed load of bombs too. As far as myself and O'Halloran can tell, there's a plot to poison the city here. I need the explosives guys and someone who deals in gaseous poisons. And the usual crowd to secure the scene."

"What the hell's going on?"

"Something large, by the looks of it. Is the Fed still there?"

"No, she is not. Apparently there's been a call taking her

away."

"Get down here Chief, and I'll fill you in on what I think is going on. What's just happened may be the thin end of the wedge."

Walking back to O'Halloran, I find him sitting on the ground, wrapping his foot in a bandage with a security guard standing over him. The guard looks shaken and is staring at the beast, which I note, hasn't moved. Well that's one good thing.

"What's your name, son?"

"Eh.., oh, Klimes, sir."

"You spoken to anyone about this yet?"

"No, I just helped this man as he was injured. But then I saw…that."

"Yes, vicious thing. Listen up! Very soon there's going to be a lot of police round because I called them. You are to stay here with Mr O'Halloran until they arrive. There have been a few deaths due to that beast, and I'm going to scout the scene to make sure the coast is clear. So stay close to O'Halloran and keep your eyes peeled. However, don't shoot any of my colleagues."

The man nods. I had forgotten that there might have been more creatures or something else. I don't have a gun either, so let's hope this walk is uneventful.

Walking back to the explosives, I find myself beginning to shake. Years in the job has allowed me to hold back the adrenalin and rage, to focus more directly on what's happening. But now the action's stopped there's a payback.

It's a neat little arrangement with the explosive packages causing a reaction to allow the resultant nasty to drift into the city. But there's also a recklessness. The gas could kill or maim anyone, totally indiscriminent. That means even their own could suffer. It takes a moment to get my head around why someone wouldn't discriminate. Their arriving demon must be worth it, whatever he promises them.

Staying well clear of the actual devices, I walk round the cylinder which they encompass and look for anything I might be missing. It takes the third time round for the writing to make itself known to me, but then again, it is dark and I am getting on. But the third time reveals a legend faintly scribed on the side of the giant vessel. It reads,

"The Darkness is coming. All hail the Darkness!"

I spit onto the ground in defiance. Well, it's one – nil to me. And that's unusual.

The ground where I have spat seems to be giving out heat as I see the spit bubble slowly evaporate. Tapping the ground with my foot, it gives back a reassuring thud, like every other piece of concrete floor I have ever tapped. Gently, I trace the edge of the hot piece of concrete and find myself drawing a circle about a human wide. I muse over what to do about this but decide there's nothing I can do except point it out to the forensics when they get here. There's too much more to do to start getting investigative at all the sites. Once the Chief is here I'll get round the other sites.

There are flashing blue lights in the distance which gives me reassurance. I walk away from the explosives before taking my mobile out and ringing Kyla.

"Hi. Is there any luck down the docks?"

"All's quiet so far, Mulgrew. We've been on the pilot boat hopping around the dock, scoping out places for them to hide their devices."

"Okay, Kyla. Did anyone check with the port authority about any last minute diversions? I reckon this must be a forced occurrence to a vessel or a scheduled arrival, something planned for months." I can hear Jenny Tatler in the background, questioning everything I am saying.

"Sure, I'll check the coastguard as well, see if there's any reports."

"And Kyla, ring me if you find any circular spots in the ground emitting heat." Ten o'clock, two hours to the apocalypse!"

45

Chapter 45

The Chief is as sceptical as hell until I show him the carcass of the beast. Bombs he's seen before, mad plots and chemical attacks, whilst rare, are not unheard of. But a creature like this takes some passing over. Forensics arrive and I show them the hot spot, but there's nothing definitive at the moment. As I have little time, I decide to plant the Chief in a corner to debrief and then get going to the other sites. As far as I can tell, this site is nailed down.

"You're telling me you went behind my back whilst there was multiple threats to the city! What were you thinking?" The Chief snorts as he finishes.

"Trouble was, sir, your Fed friend was known to me. Whilst on earlier investigation, she tried to kill me, and I thought better of it than to let her know all I know."

"Okay, if that's true, and I'm not saying I believe it, then we better get moving to these other sites."

I smile. "My guys are already there, sir, and I think we need a silent approach to this. If they see us coming, they may just do what they are going to do early."

"And you know these targets from what?" The Chief gives me the eyes that say that this time the truth better be forth coming.

"Okay, since you ask, from a nun with no eyes."

He shakes his head at me. "It's only because this one is good that I'm going with this, Trimble. And don't mention the nun to anyone else. There's the department's reputation to think of."

"I'm going to run by the cathedral, sir. Can you get onto the stadium and see what you can do there? Might be best to evacuate the place."

"You are saying midnight for these attacks? The place will be well clear by then. But I'll get down there and shake things up, see what I can find."

Nodding, I give a look-in on O'Halloran, but all I get is a dirty look as he has a go at the orderly attending to him. He's a miserable git. Taking the car, I race back into town without my lights on and have to give some keen eyed badges the heave-ho when they stop me for my speed. It's a pain when people do their job sometimes.

There's a gathering at the cathedral already, and I can see the figure of Gonzales running around. He fails to notice me, and I resort to grabbing his shoulder.

"What's happening?"

"Boss, where did you come from? I've had the place searched from top to bottom but there's nothing. It's not like there's good hiding places, lot of stone, easy to search nooks and crannies."

"What about the people coming in?"

"We have spotters on the doors who know the regulars. Anyone else is getting the special treatment, but nothing's turned up."

I peer inside the cathedral where there seems to be a bit of commotion. In the middle of the naive there are people setting up microphones and what may be a temporary stand.

"What's the big deal?"

"The Bishop wants it," answers Gonzales. "Apparently he will feel more at home speaking from the middle of the crowd. Says he prefers to be closer to the people. Tell you what, it got some of the tech guys in a tizzy changing things last minute like that."

"I'm sure. Enough going on as it is." I give Gonzales an encouraging nod and take myself into the cathedral, thinking I can scan it quickly for anything Gonzales has missed. Truth is, I don't really know what to do. I have my people deployed and now it's a wait and see. That's the problem, when things are happening it's all systems go, but now it's a case of patience. Not my forte!

Deciding to see the main players in this evening's service, I cut through to the rear of the cathedral and try to access the priest's rooms. A spritely teen steps across my way announcing that you need to be clergy to go any further. I tell him I'm on a mission from God but he fails to get the film reference and I push past, disgusted at the younger generation's lack of knowledge of the classics. There's a shout after me before a priest sticks his head out of the doorway ahead.

"Trimble. Gonzales' boss."

The priest tells the excitable chimp behind me that it's okay and then ushers me through the door.

"It's a pleasure to meet you, Officer, but it appears we have had no success. I won't cancel, mind. It's important to stand up against these things, not to be threatened."

"Of course, but try and be on the lookout too. Where's your guest?"

"He's just through here, I guess it would be a good idea for you guys to meet," suggests the priest and points me to a small door. "It's his private changing room so I would knock."

Taking the advice, I thunder out a warning and stand back from the door. My attentions would have woken the hounds of hell, and I'm a little surprised that it takes a full minute for the bishop to respond with barely an acknowledgement. It's another two before I gain admittance.

"Bishop," I say, "How are you feeling?"

"It's a bit more hectic than normal, but you can't let the dark side win with these things. Need to have a little trust."

"Indeed, Excellency, but personally a suspicious sod like myself often comes in handy. My apologies as I'm not up to date with my Vatican Who's-Who but what's your background?"

He eyes me up, weighing my rudeness with my usefulness no doubt, before answering. I have been downright rude but then, that is the point. "My son, I came from a humble background on the streets of Miami and have been blessed enough to have served in three different countries before returning to my homeland." He twists awkwardly in his colourful garb, and I wonder should I help him.

"Excellency, a hand?"

"No, no, my son. There's really no need." Well looks like a need to me. I stretch out a hand to support him. "No. Dammit, I said no."

"It's kinda warm in here, Excellency, I'm surprised you dressed up so early for the midnight mass."

He stares at me, his eyes crying out at the contemptuous

child. I spot the quick breath to relax himself. "Getting oneself ready for mass is not a matter of dressing up, my son, but then I guess you wouldn't understand."

"Indeed, Excellency," I say as he brushes past me and then past Gonzales who is coming the opposite way down the corridor.

"Boss," starts Gonzales, but I put on hand on his shoulder and a finger up to my lips. Quickly, I reach inside his jacket and withdraw his handgun. I may not be a lightweight, but years of creeping around in this job has me able to walk almost silently, yet at speed, and I use this to catch up with the Bishop. I place the gun to his head, and he immediately stops walking.

"Stand perfectly still and raise your hands. Keep them where I can see them and don't reach for anything. Any non-compliance, and I will have no hesitation in killing you. "

46

Chapter 46

"What appears to be the problem, Officer?"

"It's Detective Trimble and please keep those hands visible." I hear a sharp intake of breath behind me and momentarily curse Gonzales' surprise until another voice tells me I'm wrong.

"What are you doing to his Excellency? That's our Bishop! He's no threat. Please, Detective, put your weapon away." It's the priest of the cathedral. Poor guy is probably dropping a load and expecting a shouting from his boss. Oh well, that's tough.

"Stay back, Father! I'm afraid your Bishop is batting for the other side."

"Sir?" It's Gonzales, and he's probably well baffled. Time for him to learn a little.

"Gonzales, slowly come round to the front of my clerical friend and remove his outer garment."

"Really, Detective," says the Bishop, "these are holy vestments and should not be abused in such…"

"Shut it! Now Gonzales, and be very careful, I don't want

you setting anything off."

Gonzales moves to the front of the bishop and takes out a pen-knife. Gingerly, he cuts a slit in the front of the bishop's colourful robes. After slicing down past the wearer's belly, he stops abruptly.

"Lot of wires at this point, Boss, and a lot of explosive."

"Bomb squad, Gonzales. Get them here. But first, see if there's a quick trigger."

The bishop is starting to sweat now, rivulets running past the gun I hold at his head. I can feel myself sweating too. If he was planning to blow himself up at midnight, there must be a quick trigger if things went wrong. And if he's prepared to die, then he'll activate it.

Gonzales moves very delicately around the bishop, frisking this not-so-holy man of God with his fingertips. I have half an eye on his movements, the rest on the bishop looking for any reaction. As Gonzales kneels to frisk around the man's thighs I see a slight tensing in the bishop's forehead.

There's a knee driven into Gonzales head. A hand starts to drop towards the bishop's thigh. My ears ring with the sound of a discharged weapon. The bishop clatters off the near wall which ever so briefly explodes in a puff of white before being splattered in blood. Without thinking, I trace the bishop's head with my weapon and discharge again. There's the scream of the priest, Gonzales rolling for cover, the yells of others. And I watch the bishop until I am satisfied he is dead, that his body is no longer shaking. My hands shake, and I reach down and leave Gonzales' weapon on the floor.

"Everyone back! There is a potentially dangerous device here and I need you all to clear the building."

That's the fifth person I have killed on the job.

"I said back. Sergeant get this building clear!"

I turn and look at the wall behind me. I'm stained with him. My eyes look down at my clothes. I need to do something before my brain catches up. Gonzales is tapping my shoulder, and I just nod. The young lad's taking charge well. Clear the area, I tell him, just get everyone clear.

I'm not entirely sure where I went to, but for five minutes I didn't quite get what was happening. There were vans arriving, people being herded. Someone said something about the Chief but I don't know what. There's a coffee in my hand, but how it got here I can't remember. But I do remember him falling.

"He'd have killed over a thousand people, Boss."

I nod at Gonzales. There's no regret in my thoughts, just shock. Beside me, a man who looks like padding is a style you can't get enough of, is beginning to waddle towards the cathedral. Now that's a crap job. Although just now, mine doesn't feel any better.

"Eleven o'clock, Boss. Nothing heard from the others. I believe the Chief is coming for a brief."

I'd actually forgot. Two more places.

"When did you speak to Kyla last?" I ask Gonzales.

"I haven't. I've been tied up here."

Of course he has. I fumble for my mobile.

"Mulgrew, is this important? We have a lead." Kyla sounds pumped.

"No. Two areas clear. Go check your lead." Damn, I really could do with talking to her right now. People think you grow immune to it, but you don't. Having to take a life, especially up close like that, well let's say the cliché is right, a little bit does die of you.

"Boss, the Chief has been diverted. Apparently something's

happened up at the stadium. There's been some bombs found!"

I feel weary as I lift my head to read Gonzales' face. The kid looks worried. "What sort of bombs?" I ask.

"They said a couple had gone off killing some people. Something about the bombs being placed around the stadium, outside in an encompassing circle. They're keeping the fans inside at the moment until they can get the area checked. Chief wants you over there."

I nod and ask Gonzales to get me someone with a squad car to drop me over to the stadium. Part of me is still shaking. The Bishop's face keeps coming in and out of view, and I struggle to focus on people coming up to me. Some even offer congratulations. I mean, actual congratulations! Hardly bloody appropriate.

The sirens scream out from the car as we hurtle across town. The young officer driving me there seems too young to be out on patrol. Her hair's tied in a pony tail, a simple black hairband holding it in place.

"How long you been active, Officer?"

"A month, sir."

A damn month, and she's out in this. A damn month, and she's cast into the biggest mess this city has seen in a long time. There's a freshness in her face but also a sullen look in her eyes.

"Ask it, just ask."

"Ask what, sir?"

"Whatever's on your mind."

"Didn't they find you anything to change into? I mean, you're still covered in so much blood."

"Sorry, Officer, but they got rid of the wardrobe department. Cuts by the Mayor."

She stares at me for a moment, and I remember sarcasm doesn't come easy to locals here. It's the Irish heritage that breeds it in me. And I don't apologise.

"Sometimes…what's your name…? Kobold…well, some-times, Kobold, you don't get to take a break, sometimes it's not about one thing, and you have to keep going."

"Yes, sir, but if I can say, you look like shit."

"I was going to say at times like these you need your colleagues to boost you and help you along with a positive word, but hey, Kobold, shit will do."

She goes silent, and I hope I haven't knocked her down. It was meant to be funny as funny is about all I can do to keep me from thinking about what just happened. The siren screams on outside our car.

"Kobold, know any good tunes?"

Her lips purse, and she stares at the road ahead. "Sorry sir, I'm driving."

47

Chapter 47

"You look like hell, Trimble!"

It's a rough night as it is, and now everyone's a critic. Well that's going to have to wait as thing's need done. "What's the deal with these bombs then, Chief?"

"We've had two go off, and they seem to be caused by some sort of proximity mechanism when people get close. So far, they have only given minor wounds, but we can't let the crowds out of the stadium as we reckon the bombs are all around it."

"How big are they?"

"Well," smiles the Chief, "that's the thing. They are strong enough to take out people and cause a small amount of casualties but compared to the other plots discovered tonight they are small fry. Corstain just called in saying they had seized a boat full of explosives that would have torn the harbour apart."

"She okay? Sorry, are they okay?"

"Simmer down, they are both fine, and the back-up I sent them. I wanted you up here to get your take on what's happening, because to me it doesn't seem right. It's a pickle alright how we move people out safely, but there doesn't seem to be the catastrophic element to this situation that we saw in the others."

He's right. The tall concrete structures of the stands can't drown out the hubbub of unsettled fans inside the stadium. But this is an inconvenience at the moment, hardly a welcoming statement for this "Darkness". I'm missing something.

There's a padded man complete with helmet waddling up to the Chief and he drops an ear to hear the newcomer's news.

"Trimble, they say the bombs are defuseable, reasonably complex but very doable, it would just be a matter of time."

"That's not right. Everything was primed for midnight. Something's not right."

"Well, you crack it but I'm going to get the guys to start on defusing these in case we have to evacuate on a hurry."

I nod my acknowledgement and walk off to the back of the stadium. From there, I can see the hills, dark shades of green disappearing up high into the mountain that overlooks my city. There's a calmness up there, a peaceful lack of light in the open spaces. If I was clear enough of the stadium, instead of crabby fans I'd hear the owls and other animals scurrying in the dark. Maybe even the trees rustling in the strange breeze coming from across town. Well, until the hydro station was switched on, and it drops a deluge of water, ramming more juice into the downtown neon lights.

The drop from the hydro station is quite spectacular, but some see it as a concrete eyesore riding up the mountain. In fairness, they covered most of it with trees and bushes where the concrete drop was constructed, but you can still see plenty of the pale rock beyond which tons of water fall spectacularly into a turbine.

"It's quite something, sir."

"Yes, Kobold it is. Here's a gorgeous reservoir holding who knows how much water up there. It looks amazing when perfectly still."

"My first boyfriend took me up there. Well, my first intimate one. We swam in the reservoir before getting it on at…"

"Too much detail, Kobold. I actually liked the trees and the vastness of water."

"I always thought it made for such a view from inside the stadium. And the power of the water is immense. I read that on a tour. The walls of the drop chamber are astonishingly thick, to hold the force in."

"Indeed but can we hold the lesson? I actually came here to think." She looks crestfallen. I think she was trying to reach out to me after the "shit" comment. Well, my apologies, but I don't have any time for that.

Why hold everyone in the stadium? They found nothing inside, only outside. So what are they going to do? Does this "Darkness" manifest itself as some giant monster to consume the fans trapped in there? Do they arrive in gunships? No, the nun said bombs, explosions. So what do they hit the rats in the trap with? What's the snap that breaks their back? How do you blow them away from out here if they aren't inside?

Think, Mulgrew, think. Gas explosion, causing suffering and pain, arriving on that vessel. An anti-martyr destroying the faithful. A massive destructive force in the harbour, laying waste. They are almost biblical in proportion. Locusts, rivers of blood. First-borns, frogs, invisible armies. What else was there? The flood. How is it going to flood the earth? Shit. Not the whole earth. Just sitting ducks right under its drop.

"Kobold, the car!"

"Sir?"

"Get the damn car!" I run to the Chief. "Hydro station, the hydro. What's the time?"

"What do you mean?"

"The time?!"

"Half hour to midnight."

"Send Corstain to the Hydro. Tell her to be quiet. I think I have this."

"Trimble?"

"Do it!" I scream. "And get those bombs defused as soon as possible. You need to evacuate!" I run towards the car where Kobold has the engine running. Grabbing the door and opening it wide, I fling myself inside. "Get up to the Hydro, no lights or sirens. I see what they are doing."

"Sir," she acknowledges, and the door swings shut as we pull away at pace.

I'm sure she clipped someone as we speed out of the car park, not seriously enough to stop though. Kobold has the good sense to remain quiet and focused on her driving while we get onto the freeway and make our way towards the mountain and the hydro station. It would take a hell of an explosion to bring it down, but it would unleash all that water straight down onto the stadium. It would be like a tsunami, but from above.

"So what am I walking into, sir?" asks Kobold.

"I think they are going to blow up the hydro at midnight and let the water fall onto the stadium drowning, crushing or killing everyone inside in some way or other. It's a sacrifice to a demon that's arriving tonight."

Kobold looks at me. "Demon?"

"Well, entity, demon, spirit, I don't know exactly, but there's someone dealing with it. We're just getting on top of the physical side of things. The cult that's bringing this entity to us is planning a celebration—a black one. They tried to create a toxic gas leak in the industrial zone which would have contaminated the city, they were going to massacre a load of worshippers at one of the cathedrals, wreck the harbour with a massive bomb and now they will destroy the stadium and everyone in it. I know it sounds mad, but Kobold, trust me mad just got normal."

There's a slight shake in her hands, and I notice the small cross hanging from her neck. At least she might not think I'm insane.

"So what's the plan?"

"Plan? I only just clocked their idea, and I'm praying it's the right one otherwise another disaster is going to happen that I don't know about. We get there, arm up and see if we can stop whatever's there."

Kobold cocks an eyebrow. "Whatever?"

"Yeah, whatever. There was a beast at the industrial plant. Arm up well."

There's an audible gulp from her. She's unnaturally staring at the road, forcing her nerves down.

"Ever fired in anger, Kobold?"?"

"Yes, once. Just a covering shot, though."

"Well, acquire the target, aim and damn well shoot, 'cause these people won't hesitate to kill you. And don't worry, you'll be fine."

I hope she can't see through the lie, but I need her calm and thinking. Kyla will be on her way too with Jenny Tatler. How come when I'm walking into my possible death, the woman I loved and the one I now want to spend my life with, end up here too?

Kobold turns off the main road and finds the service road up to the hydro.

"Kill your lights. Let's hope no one sees us coming."

Chapter 48

"See anything?"

Kobold shakes her head, and I lean round the corner briefly scouring the darkness. She's left her police cap in the car and is holding her handgun pointed down. Her blonde ponytail flips around as she keeps checking our rear. There's a tension in the air and I am feeling the nerves myself which is fairly unusual.

There's a flash of red in the distance, and I try to see what's moving. Behind that moment of colour, there are shadows, and I cannot tell the source as clouds are blocking the moonlight and I also suspect these individuals, whoever they are, are wearing black. I turn to Kobold. who is staring at me wide eyed. Mouthing "Was that someone?" I get an exaggerated nod and the word "Twelve" was mouthed back. A dozen! Bollocks. Where's Kyla?

We are crouched at the corner of the main hydro building, and before us is the reservoir, set up as a large lake with a solid sandstone colour wall penning it in. There are warning signs about drowning and not climbing the wall and indications of a sheer drop. Unfortunately the bombs are probably along that wall.

There's a rustle behind us, and Kobold swings around, arms rising in a triangle with her gun at the point, seeking a target. A bird call can be heard, but it turns slightly flat at its end. Kobold flicks her eyes at me and sees I'm waving her gun down. Jenny Tatler, you never could hold a note!

Kyla emerges from the bushes behind us, running in a low crouch, before pinning herself flat against the wall beside me. Damn, it's good to see her. Dressed in black jeans and a jumper, she looks a better sight than myself, caked dried blood covering my clothing and face. She mouths "Alright?" I nod. "Bombs?" Turning, I indicate the wall. Her face looks perplexed until the motive dawns on her. Her eyes widen with shock and sudden terror.

Kyla draws close to my ear. "How many are here?"

"We counted twelve," I whisper back.

"I'll do a sweep and come back."

"Okay but hurry, it's ten minutes to midnight."

She doesn't look back and I watch her dark hair swinging by her neck disappear into the bushes. If that's the last view then it's a damn good one. A face looks back from the bushes. It's Jenny Tatler and I indicate her to come over to us. After all, who knows if anyone is patrolling. She's only forensics, wouldn't stand a chance.

Jenny is shaking as she arrives beside me. I guess she's rarely in this sort of situation. Taking a small handgun I stashed in my leg holster, I offer it, but she shakes her head. When I question this decision with raised eyebrows, she pulls a handgun from behind her, probably tucked into her jeans. It's got significantly more stopping power than mine. One of

Kyla's, no doubt.

For two minutes, I continue to pop my head around the building's corner and see little movement. Another minute, and I'll need to make a move anyway. Come on Kyla, where are you?

There's a brief rustle of leaves, and she's beside me. I feel her hair tickle my neck as she whispers in my ear.

"There's only eight now." Wow, she's efficient. "There's no one on the wall, as I guess that will crumble, but that's where the explosives are. It's a straight forward timer from what I could see, and there's no indications of a remote detonator. Looks like it's a case of getting to it and defusing it."

"Okay. Get Jenny to a safe location so she can provide cover. Then I'll storm the wall with Kobold, and you can stop them coming after us. Don't hold back. Remember these guys were going to sacrifice children."

Kyla nods and disappears again with Jenny. I check my watch and give her one minute. Whispering my plan to Kobold, she doesn't look overly impressed, but it's too late for a conference.

Ten seconds, be ready Kyla!

I turn to Kobold, my left hands raised counting down with my fingers. Five… four…three…two…one… My hand drops.

Kobold catches me napping as she takes the lead, rushing over to the steps and up to the wall. I vault up them behind her, and already there's cries in the air. My heart skips a beat as a shot rings out, but there's no thud or ricochet heard. Concentrating on keeping my legs moving, I struggle to keep up with Kobold who is streaking ahead along the wall. Beside me, the water laps against the pale structure and on the other side is a twelve foot drop to grass.

I allow myself a quick turn of the head and see a dark figure fall to the ground. There's flashes of gunfire from the other side of the water, and I hear Kyla calling out to Jenny to keep her head down. There's a horrible scream of pain from someone and unholy cries of vengeance.

It takes over two minutes to run the length of the wall from our starting position. I thank God that they didn't build it any longer as my lungs are giving out.

"Kobold, look at the sides. Can you see the explosives?"

I can't make out her reply, but she's now running along the width of the reservoir. A glance to the side shows me a drop unimaginable down the mountain, obviously where the water builds it's energy before hitting the turbine. There's a swirling wind up here, and I can't keep a confident pace.

Kobold suddenly pulls up and points down the dry side of the wall. Dropping to her knees, she studies over the edge. The gunfire continues, and I try to block out the risk of being exposed out here. Finally, I catch up with Kobold, and she is pulling her mobile from her pocket. I look over the edge and nearly swoon at the drop, fighting to steady myself on the wall. Although a few metres thick, to see the bombs, we need to lean over the edge.

Flat on her belly now, Kobold is moving her mobile around the device she has located on the wall and is talking to someone. I grab her legs, hoping to secure her position. For a minute, she looks intently whist I try to juke over her shoulder to see what's happening.

"I can do this, sir! I need another minute."

"Good, quick as you can," I shout. There's less gunfire now, but a shot skims off the wall beside me.

"Mulgrew, no! Mulgrew!"

It's Kyla, and I look up quickly to someone in a red monk's

habit before me. From the hands, it appears to be a woman, and this is confirmed as she pulls back her cowl to reveal curly red hair and wild green eyes that I recognise so well. She drops her hands and my mind reels as snakes appear from inside her sleeves. Behind her, I see Kyla running, weapon raised.

"Ha! Your woman…watch her die!"

The woman turns and releases a snake from within her sleeve. It hardens into a straight line, like an arrow, racing towards Kyla. There's a look of horror and then an instinctive turn before the snake pierces her side. Her body crumples, and she tumbles sideways into the reservoir.

49

Chapter 49

"Kyla!"

Her body crashes into the water, and I move to go after her. Kobold starts to slip forward, presumably because she's overstretched, and I have to keep on her legs to stop her from falling to her death.

"Now, then Detective, what are you going to do? Avenge your lover? She was your lover, wasn't she? Beautiful in her way, but without the raw power I have. Save her if you can from the devil's bite, but then your friend will die, falling to her doom before we all follow her. Hail the Darkness!"

And the red-headed woman starts to laugh, wickedly. My mind races. Kyla, *I need to save Kyla, but Kobold needs me. The City needs me!*

"How long, Kobold?"

"Shush, I'm listening to the techie."

I look up at the habit-clad woman and see her glaring back at me. I swear her eyes change into narrow slits like a snake. Bending down, the wind billowing her habit, she lets loose several snakes from her sleeves. They slither towards me, forcing a natural recoil. From the corner of my eye, I see Kyla floating motionless, face down in the water.

"And now my dears will immobilise you, and I'll watch your body fall below. I'll kick your little bitch over with you before seeing this flood happen on the stadium below. Thousands dead, Detective, all from your ineptitude, all on your hands. And he shall lift me up for praising him in such a beautiful fashion."

Again she laughs, and I'm stranded, unable to do anything lest Kobold falls.

"Thirty seconds, Detective!"

I close my eyes as the snakes reach my hands, determined to hold onto Kobold with everything I have. The woman is shrieking wildly at my predicament, encouraging on her beasts.

A single gunshot. I open my eyes to see blood spurt from the woman's shoulder. Then two more pierce her arm and then her leg. There's a flash of colour behind her, and I see her tumble sideways off the wall. She thumps off the wall before I lose sight of her. Snakes bite into my fingers. And then I hear Kobold scream in delight.

Jenny Tatler appears in front of me, grabbing the end of a snake but it refuses to let go of my finger, and I scream out as she places her gun at the end of my palm. There's a piercing pain as I see her fling the snake clear after the awful crack of gunshot. My ears ring, and I see her stumble. She grabs hold of my leg as she falls before grabbing the end of the other snake. Again she pulls her trigger, and I scream out.

What's left of my hands are free, and I feel Kobold pushing herself back up onto the wall. There's been no explosion and something in the back of my mind says "Job done" but the foremost part is racing. I dive into the water and swim to Kyla. There's no movement from her. There's a splash behind me, and Jenny's there turning Kyla over.

The water's deep, and I have to kick hard to stay upright in order to support Kyla. I scream at her face to talk to me. Jenny is grabbing her neck, checking pulse maybe. I'm turning cold, numb. The water around me is turning a slight red, visible even in the darkness of this night.

There's shouting from Kobold, yelling for help into her mobile. Jenny is screaming at me to help get Kyla out of the water. There's tears streaming down my face, and I can taste their bitterness when they reach my lips. But I kick hard under the water and slowly we move back to the wall.

Then I'm on my knees, watching Jenny astride Kyla, trying to force air into her lungs. And there's a helicopter above us. Kobold's yelling at Jenny that we need to move Kyla because of the down draught and our proximity to the drop. Jenny's swearing back and telling them to get on with it. It feels like forever before I see Kyla disappearing into the night sky with Jenny in the back of the chopper.

Kobold has to walk me back carefully along the wall. I'm swooning and unsure if I am hearing voices or if people are talking to me. A red stain has formed on Kobold's jacket which is wrapped around my hands.

"It's okay, sir. She's gone into the best of care. They have her. And we won."

I stare at her wondering how this is winning. My hands scream at me. The woman I love is fighting for her life. And who knows what's happened to the nun? Who knows?

The paramedic takes off Kobold's jacket and begins to attend to my wounds. There's a mask shoved over my face, and I draw in large gulps of air that is better for me than that around me. A win? I blew a man's brains out. I nearly lost everyone that helped me.

"Trimble, good work," says the Chief. "Bomb squad are mighty impressed with young Kobold there." I give him a questioning look. "She was dangling over a massive drop using her camera phone to get disarming instructions from our bomb guys. If she hadn't, I'd be dead right now along with nearly a hundred thousand more people. It's after midnight so I guess that's it all done."

"Yes sir." The paramedic places me into the back of the ambulance and is about to shut the door. "Kobold," I shout.

"I have to help wrap this up, sir."

"Go with him," says the Chief. "Make sure no one comes after him."

Kobold jumps into the back of the ambulance, is joined by the paramedic, and we are on our way. There's no siren, so I mustn't be too bad. Although this happy thought is tainted by the revelation that my fingers weren't found. It's funny, I can almost feel them.

Chapter 50

It's been three days. After they patched up my fingers, or rather where the gaps where, they let me come down and sit with Kyla. Her long hair was greasy and bedraggled after coming out of the water, and her face showed serious bruising. Yet that was nothing compared to the silence in the room, punctuated only by an occasional blip from the machines and her rasping breath.

That was my company as I refused to leave the room. Sure, the Chief came in, Gonzales, a recovered Hughes and even Jenny Tatler asking what I had done to her colleague. It'll probably be the last night we let the forensics crowd out with us. It might have been a last night for a lot of things.

On his second visit the Chief told me they were still searching for the body of the snake woman in the red habit. They had scoured everywhere and there wasn't even an indication of where she had fallen. At times, I can still see the eyes burning into me, like a wanton evil. The Chief laughed when I said I didn't believe she was dead.

But there was a greater worry on my mind. We had stopped

the physical disasters, but we weren't the only ones fighting that night. As I sat holding Kyla's hand, I told her all about the nun, all the things that had happened and of my admiration for her. And of my fear of what had happened. The priest was still missing as well. A boy from his congregation visited with flowers for Kyla, but he had no news of the Father's return.

I suffered the coffee machine in the hall for a day before I rang Gonzales to go and get something decent. He offered to wait with Kyla while I got some air, but I couldn't leave her.

It's the third day, and I'm still here beside Kyla. The bright blue of the room is becoming depressing, and I think the air of disinfectant is finally subduing me. From the window at the end of the room, I can see across the city. The stadium is just about in sight and there's only faint reminders of the panic of the earlier night. Two police cars sit out front with a couple of beat guys moving on anyone staying too long.

There's a rustle behind me, and I turn and see Kyla's hand squeezing the covers, the plastic undersheets making the foreign sound. Her head rolls slightly, and I race over, taking her hand in mine. I drop my face in front of hers looking for any movement, and my heart jumps as her eyes slowly open into a squint.

"Kyla? Can you hear me, Kyla?"

There's a nod, and she moves her head at a snail's pace to survey the room. From the flowers to the monitor to the banks of equipment, she gradually soaks it all in. Then a sudden panic races across her face and she looks at me questioningly.

"My legs. Mulgrew, I can't feel them."

***

They took her away before coming back to confirm that her legs simply don't work anymore. Medically they can't work out why. But then it may not be a medical problem. Who knows what those snakes did to her? And I begin to feel gratitude for losing my fingers. Standing with the doctor as he delivers his assessment, I can feel someone's gaze burning into the back of my head. Turning, I see a familiar face sitting in a wheelchair. Her eyeless face is freaking out several people, but there's a thin smile as I approach.

"You did it. Thank God, you did it. But at a price." Her hands take mine, and she traces where my fingers should have been. "I'm sorry."

"It's not a lot. Kyla's lost the use of her legs. No one knows why but…"

"It won't be the last sacrifice."

"Did you…?"

She drops her head into her hands almost convulsing. Her voice drags in sharp breaths like she is sobbing, but there are no eyes to cry her tears. I wait for her, but she keeps tilting her head away from me like she is ashamed.

"What is it?"

"God forgive me. But it was stronger than I imagined. Our friend the priest didn't survive. I barely did. To be face to face with…such evil. God help this city. Trimble, it's here, and it will breed!"

With that, she's taken away, wounds to be dealt with. How strong was this thing if she couldn't deal with it? I'm at a loss to imagine.

Taking a stroll to the elevator, I ride to the top of the hospital tower and find the steps to the roof. There's a low hanging grey cloud, and the drizzle makes me feel slightly cold. The whirr of the cooling towers for the air conditioning is my only companion except for the pigeons. Standing at the edge, I stare down at the city.

He won't have it. This thing that's arrived won't get to rule this place. I grew up here, and I'll die defending it. This "Darkness" will not prevail. I'll heal and seek it out to destroy it. And I'll stand with whoever will stand with me. This is my city. I am its pastor, and I will help clear its unsatisfactory habits away. But for now…coffee!

About the Author

GR Jordan is a self-published author who finally decided at forty that in order to have an enjoyable lifestyle, his creative beast within would have to be unleashed. His books mirror that conflict in life where acts of decency contend with self-promotion, goodness stares in horror at evil and kindness blind-sides us when we are at our worst. Corrupting our world with his parade of wondrous and horrific characters, he highlights everyday tensions with fresh eyes whilst taking his methodical, intelligent mainstays on a roller-coaster ride of dilemmas, all the while suffering the banter of their provocative sidekicks.

A graduate of Loughborough University where he masqueraded as a chemical engineer but ultimately played American football, GR Jordan worked at changing the shape of cereal flakes and pulled a pallet truck for a living. Watching vegetables freeze at -40'C was another career highlight and he was also one of the Scottish Highlands' "blind" air traffic controllers. Having flirted with most places in the UK, he is now based in the Isle of Lewis in Scotland where his free time is spent between raising a young family with his wife, writing, figuring out how to work a loom and caring for a small flock of chickens. Luckily his writing is influenced by his varied work and life experience as the chickens have not been the poetical inspiration he had hoped for!

You can connect with me on:
- http://www.grjordan.com
- https://www.twitter.com/carpetless
- https://www.facebook.com/carpetlessleprechaun

Subscribe to my newsletter:
- http://grjordan.com/download-footsteps

Also by G R Jordan

G R Jordan writes Urban Fantasy and Dark Fantasy books in several series, including the Austerley & Kirkgordon series. At the time of publishing there are 3 origin stories and 3 full length novels with more planned in the near future. Published books are detailed below, including the feel good fantasy series, Island Adventures.

Crescendo!: An Austerley & Kirkgordon Adventure #1
A shape-shifting dragon. A cult bringing forth a nightmare. Two broken men, separated by hatred, must bind together to save the world.

Bitter-sweet partners, Austerley and Kirkgordon, take on the darkness to prevent a displaced people ending the world. If you like bizarre creatures, fast paced action and cataclysmic nightmares, you'll love G R Jordan's first novel. Get the book readers have called "a fast paced gothic thriller with lots of humour" and "refreshingly modern take on Lovecraftian themes."

Can the Elder darkness be stopped? It's the blasphemous fanfare for the end of the world!

The Darkness at Dillingham: An Austerley & Kirkgordon Adventure #2

An exhibitionist witch. A English seaside town literally descending to hell. And the only hope is a broken partnership that doesn't want to heal!

"The Darkness at Dillingham" is the second instalment in the A&K urban fantasy series. If you like breakneck action, sexy villains and cutting dialogue, then you'll love this misfit set of heroes. Can the team bind together long enough to rescue a cursed town? Get the book one reader called "A real roller coaster of spookiness with some sexy bits thrown in".

Dillingham, the nightlife's straight from hell!

Dagon's Revenge: An Austerley & Kirkgordon Adventure #3

A shattered hero races to save his wife. A rescue team falling apart. Elder god Dagon's coming back and he's pissed!

Kirkgordon takes his team beyond our world in this third instalment in the Austerley & Kirkgordon urban fantasy series. If you like danger and desire, punchy dialogue and cataclysmic nightmares then you'll love G R Jordan's bunch of discombobulated heroes.

Sometimes, there are no good choices!

Footsteps: Austerley & Kirkgordon Origins #1

An insane professor. A journey into a New England grave. Will Kirkgordon return alive?

It was supposed to be a quiet protection job. But under a New England grave yard Kirkgordon meets his worst nightmares. Will he make it out alive with his protectee? Or will he kill him, himself?

Kirkgordon gets his first taste of dark creatures in this first origin story from the A&K universe. If like you like action and adventure, dark creatures from beyond and cutting dialogue from antagonistic heroes then you'll love G R Jordan's A&K urban fantasy series.

Is the real madness above or below the surface?

Cally: Austerley & Kirkgordon Origins #2

A village emptied of its children. A warrior finding her greatest desire. But a witch's vengeance wrecks a curse that will devastate her forever.

The tale of Calandra's curse is the 2nd story in the A&K origins series, a collection of short stories that expand G R Jordan's A&K universe. If you love rollicking action, imperfect heroes and extraordinary, magical villains, then you will love the Austerley & Kirkgordon series.

Yesterday, he offered her the rest of his life. Today a vengeful witch wants to take him away. Can Calandra's dreams survive the mother of all storms?

Sometimes a woman can be too cold for any man!

The People in the Pool: Austerley & Kirkgordon Origins #3
He lost her, murdered a long time ago. But now she's returned. If something isn't real, does it matter?

"The People in the Pool" is the 3rd origin story in the A&K origins series, a collection of short stories that expand G R Jordan's A&K universe. If you love rollicking action, imperfect heroes and weird villains and places, then you will love the Austerley & Kirkgordon series.

Not every mother can warm a child's heart.

Surface Tensions: Island Adventures #1

Mermaids sighted near a Scottish island. A town exploding in anger and distrust. And Donald's got to get the sexiest fish in town, back in the water.

"Surface Tensions" is the first story in a series of Island adventures from the pen of G R Jordan. If you love comic moments, cosy adventures and light fantasy action, then you'll love these tales with a twist.

Get the book that amazon readers said, "perfectly captures life in the Scottish Hebrides" and that explores "human nature at its best and worst".

Something's stirring the water!